Another Day in the Life

Another Day in the Life

Published 2014 by arima publishing

www.arimapublishing.com

ISBN 978 1 84549 623 4

A catalogue record of this book is available from the British Library

arima publishing
ASK House, Northgate Avenue
Bury St Edmunds, Suffolk IP32 6BB
t: (+44) 01284 700321

www.arimapublishing.com

Another Day in the Life
Extraordinary Real Life Stories

Contents

Introduction

Following the success of *A Day in the Life,* First de Sales is pleased to present a second collection of amazing, amusing and astounding real life stories from a selection talented authors all of whom were specially invited to contribute to this book.

Another Day in the Life is an eclectic collection of stories that in one form or another touch upon family or close personal relationships. Whether comic, quirky or tragic, each story is beautifully written and perfectly encapsulates the author's emotions and thoughts.

As you would expect with a De Sales book, within this anthology occurs a spectrum of experience. There is a hair-raising encounter with Hitler's barber, a desperate battle to save a girl's life, the flat with its uninvited resident and pitched battles on the troubled streets of Belfast.

This is a book that offers the full range of human experience and emotion. *Another Day in the Life* will entertain, inform and stimulate the reader from cover to cover.

- 1 -

A Soldier of Fortune

I can't remember when my parents stopped living with each other. It's all a bit vague. They had been arguing for at least three years. It was always in the other room so that we didn't hear the verbal abuse being hurled at one and other.

I do know, however, that on the night of the Northern Ireland Internment in August 1971, nobody was looking after my brother John and me. We were supposedly staying with Peter (not his real name), a young man who worked for my father. I didn't like staying there because he always walked around the house in a pair of old pyjamas which revealed all too much; I would turn away in timidly in disgust. I had my suspicions as to what he was trying to do but I was only ten so, like so many things at that age, it passed me by.

This night in Belfast was different though. There was a huge amount of army movement in the streets. A Saracen jeep pulled up at the bottom of the hill and the Paras jumped out to set up a roadblock. There was an immediate local reaction as the neighbours began the customary bin lid banging to alert all around. The Brits were here and the protesters needed to man the barricades.

Peter wasn't around for some reason. Maybe he could not get through the mass of protesters who had hi-jacked cars, lifted the paving slabs and set up a small innocuous fortification. We sneaked out and John and I immediately headed for the nearest group of youths. They was an buzz of excitement as more teenagers came from all directions. Whistles shrilled and car horns were continually pressed.

Whatever the Internment was, it had ignited a spark and the people were called to arms. I followed the crowd as they surged down the hill, throwing bottles, bricks. Then a Molotov cocktail lit up the sky as it hurled through the night air. It missed but still everyone cheered.

The soldiers remained calm despite their young years. The troop carrier then slowly moved on to the great delight of the home crowd. A small victory. The excitement abated and mothers suddenly appeared form the small terraced houses and dragged their children back home.

When we woke we immediately looked out to see what scars remained. The charred remains of an old

Volkswagen Beetle still smouldered and the younger children were stoning it as if they were in battle. We needed to find out where everyone was. The older youths were probably still in their pits having consumed a few too many beers. Women went about their usual business, stopping to discuss the night before. What were we going to do until the fight restarted?

We tried to play football but the usual pitch was laden with broken paving slabs and milk bottles. It was the munitions dump for the oncoming onslaught. This was boring but then the word came through that the Dublin Road was the place to be. About eight of us manfully headed off towards the other side of town. As we reached the bottom of Bridge Street, we could see ahead the hazy movement of a small crowd. As we drew near we saw them systematically lifting the paving stones, carrying them back up the hill and breaking them. Another munitions dump. The closer we got the more we saw that this group was made up of more adults than we had seen the previous night. Maybe they had been hiding in case they had were arrested in the mass raid which netted some 300-350 unsuspecting 'terrorists'.

It was nearly midday and the staff of the nearby Unemployment Office were seen closing up 'the Dole' for fear of riotous behaviour. Some of them turned right and back down into the town, whereas a handful came to join the revolution.

We kept breaking up the pavements in anticipation of our assault on the British Forces. We were going to send them home and force the release our jailed heroes.

Another hour past and the crowd grew to about 250 fervent protesters, but still no sign of the enemy. I was hungry so we went up to the garage to get some sweets. The owner's son knew us so we were able to pick and choose what we wanted without paying the full amount.

As I picked up a packet of crisps I heard the sound of the crowd rise: the army had arrived. I ran back down the hill to the front of the barricade and manfully picked up a stone. The crowd jeered as the soldiers jumped out of their jeeps. A Sergeant briefed his Captain and they seemed content to simply survey the scene. No real threat seemed to exist and thus the troops remained calm. These weren't the Paras, they were another Brigade and so nobody really was concerned. The Paras were the bad boys.

Another 30 minutes passed without any sign of movement and we stood jeering the soldiers below. There were still over 200 insurgents waiting for the moment.

Then suddenly from behind the Saracens, a group of maybe thirty Paras emerged. We knew it was them because of their uniform and their long batons. They began their advance and picked up speed. I grabbed another stone and stood firm on top of the small pile of paving slabs.

The soldiers drew closer and I threw my first missile. It was far off the mark and so I bent down to gather more.

The soldiers were nearly upon us but for some reason I could not see any other flying missiles. As I bent down I looked behind me for reassurance from my fellow rioters. But as I turned I realised that they all had fled! I had been abandoned by my fellow protesters; the insurgents had been beaten even before a hail of stones had been thrown in anger.

I looked back in the direction of the soldiers. They were nearly upon me. What was I to do? Should I run?

I froze. I was somewhat placed over to the left of the road and thus the main troop surged past in chase of the fleeing rioters. However, two huge soldiers were running towards me, batons outstretched. What were they going to do? I felt a fear that I had never felt before. But it was too late: they were upon me. I stood motionless holding the two stones tightly in my sweaty hands.

As they came upon me they brushed past, one on either side, but made no attempt to make me pay for my riotous behaviour. They rushed on up the hill in pursuit but left me standing. I had not been punished. I was trembling like never before. They had let me go. For why, I did not know but the relief was palatable. I dropped the stones and got down off the small mound. My political and revolutionary career was over. I was, at the age of ten, a retired soldier of fortune.

- 2 -

Guilt and Innocence

ACT I

The clock on the wall of the interview room read 03:24 in green neon numerals. We were now on our third recorded interview tape; and the third caution that my responses could be used in any subsequent criminal trial. Of course I was not actually under arrest, nor had I yet been charged with any offence, but there was no doubt from the approach of the interviewing detectives that things were very serious. Very serious indeed.

They asked when I had last seen my father alive. I responded that I left him around 7 pm on Saturday evening. Of course there was no proof of the exact time, as he lived in a fairly remote country location with none of the surveillance cameras seen in urban areas or on main roads which would have recorded my movements and confirmed my story. I was able to confirm that I arrived at my hotel just before 8 pm as the receptionist was able to support that. The hotel was fifty miles away, so the timings seemed about right.

'Did you leave the hotel any time that evening?' asked the detective.

I replied that I had arrived at the hotel planning to pop out for a drink later but, as I had just started the symptoms of a minor but persistent head cold, had decided instead to get an early night. The detective wryly observed that there was therefore nobody who could support my whereabouts from 8 pm until checkout time the following day. I suggested that there may be some security cameras in the hotel and the detective was quick to point out that my room was on the ground floor, and that I could have easily avoided the cameras by leaving through the large open window.

'Did you tell your wife that you were staying at a hotel that night?' This was the next question. It was one that I knew would be coming and to which I had no convincing answer.

'No,' I replied. 'The reason I went to Milton Keynes because a shop there stocked something that she wanted for Christmas. As I wanted it to be a surprise present, I didn't tell her.'

'So where did she think you were on Saturday night and Sunday morning?' asked the Detective. I replied that I had led my wife to believe that I stayed at my father's house that evening. This elicited another difficult question.

'So you wanted to secretly stay overnight, just an hour from your father's home so you could do some Christmas shopping? You could easily have just popped along the following morning from your father's house without the expense of a hotel. You do often stay with your father at his house do you not?'

I could not deny that it sounded odd. Why would I leave the comfort of my father's home, where I would often stay a couple of nights per week, to go Christmas shopping less than an hour away? And without telling anyone? And especially given my current financial position?

Ah yes. The financial position.

'Do you have any brothers or sisters?'

I replied that I was an only child and confirmed that my mother had died some years earlier.

'Would you describe your father as wealthy?'

I responded rather lamely that I was unsure what was meant by 'wealthy', but that he was probably best described as comfortably off.

I was fearful of what their next question might be. I was not wrong.

'And you, Mr Phillips. Are you comfortably off?'

And thus my dilemma was unfolded. I explained about the big tax bill, the financial problems after my divorce, and the loans which my father had generously extended to me to help until things got sorted out. There was little point in concealment as all would surely become apparent under further investigation.

This was not going well, not well at all. This was clearly evidenced by the expressionless faces of the two detectives. Even 'good cop' seemed to be stiffening his posture whilst my principal interrogator was already eying up the charge sheet.

ACT II

It was the early hours of Monday morning, and the clock clicked round to 03:30.

I had arrived back at my father's house around 6 pm Sunday evening after failing to get my wife's Christmas present in Milton Keynes because it was out of stock. I was met by flashing blue lights in the early chill of the mid-December evening. The policeman told me that my father's dead body had been found in his home earlier Sunday afternoon, the result of a violent attack.

Shortly afterwards the detectives had arrived and, whilst expressing sympathy and sensitivity for my loss, were quick to point out that their primary investigative obligation was to my dead father, and to use the time immediately following his death to establish as many facts as possible as quickly as possible. In that regard they would like to interview me immediately if I would agree. I did.

Nine hours later. The third cautioned interview tape was being unloaded and sealed in a signed bag as evidence. They had asked if they could take my mobile phone, my laptop and my car away for analysis. They asked me to hand over my clothes and shoes for forensic tests.

My wife had been called by the police to bring a change of clothes to a local hotel where we were to stay pending further interrogation the following morning. She was distraught at the loss of my father but even more so at the surreal picture she saw unfolding.

Why had I not told her the truth about going to Milton Keynes? She trusted me and believed in me but could I please, please, absolutely promise her that my father and I had not argued and things got out of control?

I barely slept the remaining few hours of that fateful night. As the police interrogation had palpably revealed, I had behaved in a very odd way in going secretively to a hotel with no supportable alibi. The last time anyone other than me was able to say my father was alive was when he went shopping at 1 pm on Saturday. His body was found by a passing neighbour on Sunday afternoon leaving me a full 24 hours of opportunity to have killed him. Not just the opportunity but also a motive, as I was patently financially stressed with significant obligations to my father.

For the first time in my life, I could see that a reasonable man might easily conclude that I was potentially the most heinous of murderers. And I could not have blamed him.

ACT III

The following interview session did not begin until late afternoon.

The police were busy following up on house-to-house calls, forensics, appealing for witnesses, etc. My wife and I stayed holed up in our hotel, both terrified to speak about what was really occupying our minds as our stomachs churned. Partly over the tragedy of my dear father but mostly out of fear that I was the prime suspect in the investigation and was incapable of providing any convincing rebuttal.

At 5 pm on Monday I was steeled for the next body blow when my life, which had been turned upside down in the previous 24 hours was about, yet again, to be tossed by the troubled sea of fortune.

The police had found my father's missing car, abandoned by those who stole it during their getaway from his home. A witness said that the car had been abandoned between 10.30 and 11 pm on Saturday night.

In the way that buses seem to arrive all at once, hope emerged with another unscripted and entirely random revelation.

It was then revealed that my father's best friend had spoken with him on the telephone around 9.15 pm on Saturday. Amazingly the hotel at which I had stayed in Milton Keynes confirmed that whilst the ground floor windows did open, they were restricted, and did not open wide enough for anything other than a hamster to escape during the night. Described rather condescendingly by my tailor as 'a short portly', a nimble rodent I am not!

ACT IV

All at once it seemed that, however absurd my story had sounded, my father was proven to be alive an hour after I had arrived at the hotel. The security cameras at the hotel, coupled with the window aperture, confirmed I did not venture from my room until the following day. During this time my father's car had been stolen and abandoned and his dead body discovered.

In the days that followed more and more good old fashioned detective work pieced together evidence which ultimately led to the charge of two individuals who confessed to violent robbery and were imprisoned for murder.

Sometimes, when I am ever contemplative about life, I am reminded about the way in which seemingly unimportant combinations of facts are so life changing when juggled together by fate.

A few innocent but suspicious facts could have labelled me a potential murderer, whereas a timely phone call and a restricted window aperture made me innocent again.

Guilty and Innocent – a life sentenced in 24 hours.

- 3 -

Hitler's Barber

I was twelve years old in the summer of 1978, spending my second summer at the large country house of a family relation whose connection to me is too convoluted to describe. In the week before leaving America I had been given a decent haircut but, after only eight weeks in Germany, my aunt decided that my shoulder-length hair most definitely needed further trimming.

During a shopping trip to the neighbouring market town, she gave me fifteen deutschemarks and dropped me off at a high street barbershop that had seen better days. I was left in the waiting area on my own, as my aunt attended to her errands around the town. In the waiting area I was surrounded by four elderly men who were chatting amiably with the three barbers about local trivia that did not interest me in the slightest.

When the chair at the end of the row became available, I climbed into it, to find that my assigned barber was a good thirty years older than the other men in the room. He was perhaps eighty or eighty-five years old, with unkempt white hair and shaky hands that made him wholly unsuitable to the task of cutting hair. His demeanour was friendly enough and, seeing that I was a very young, impressionable boy, he immediately began to regale me with a well-worn story about how he had cut Hitler's hair when he was working in nearby Braunschweig during the 1920s. The other barbers vouched for his story, although it was clear to me that they were in no position to judge, not least because of they were one generation too young.

Although I was historically literate enough to know that Hitler had acquired German citizenship in Braunschweig at around the time of the barber's story, I remained unconvinced. My immediate concern was with the barber's shaky hands and his lack of attention to the task of cutting my hair. His scissors were lopping off tufts of my hair at odd angles as he repeatedly turned to his audience seated behind the two of us, seeking confirmation of this or that detail in his story.

His cutting was done and I could see in the mirror that my former blond shoulder-length hair had become a crazy quilt of patches. Despite of the clear incompetence shown by the man, I paid him his fee; it would be a few years before I had the confidence to stand up to an elderly group of strangers and argue in a foreign language.

Outside the shop, I was reunited with my aunt, who made a very unconvincing effort to declare that my new, extremely short haircut suited me well. I recognised it as a very feeble attempt the minimise her own sense of guilt in deciding to send me to Hitler's barber. Indeed, even several weeks after the event, I had trouble convincing my own mother that I hadn't cut my own hair in order to keep the fifteen marks for myself.

This had been far and away the worst haircut of my life, and I spent the rest of the summer trying to grow it out, and to repair the asymmetric tufts that extended over one ear but not the other, and to taper my fringe so that it no longer attracted the stares of whoever I was talking to. It was not until late September that I felt confident enough to attend school without the concealment provided by an upturned collar.

In spite of, or maybe because of my aunt's disastrous choice of barbers, she was a great hostess in other respects. I was given use of a motorbike despite my young age, with which I could roam the farm tracks around the vast estate. I was also introduced to alcohol, in the form of a fruit punch that produced a dramatic collision between myself and a glass door, which I won decisively.

My barbershop experience was not the only occasion in which I encountered older Germans with rum opinions about events before the war, but on account of a bad haircut, this one stayed with me more than the others.

- 4 -

Early Daze

I have only fleeting recollections of my life before five or six years old and cannot even picture my father whom my mother divorced sometime between my fifth and sixth birthdays.

I know we returned to Hull where I was born, and I resumed school there for a time until World War Two began. It was a most confusing time in my life as I had no concept of war or what it would mean for me. I soon found out.

One day I was happily going to school and coming to terms with my new life, and the next I was standing nervously with lots of other bewildered kids and weeping parents on the platform at Paragon Station. I was holding a little suitcase and a cardboard box containing a strange object which I was told was a gas mask, and might one day save my life; so I held on to it very tightly. Apparently I was being 'evacuated' and my despair at what this might entail soon changed to delight when I discovered it was not to some unknown, scary destination but to Scarborough where I had spent a memorable holiday the year before. My grandparents had a four bedroom house there on the north side and I was going to live with them.

Aunt Helen, mum's younger sister, also lived with us as her husband was in the Merchant Navy and away a lot. I was sad to learn that grandfather had to stay in Hull, where he was the senior maths master at one of the city's grammar schools, but he came back every Friday and all school holidays. He was a larger than life character and I came to regard him more and more like the father figure I needed.

Scarborough was supposed to be safer than Hull but I eventually experienced more action there than I would have had back home. I remember lying in bed nearly every night, hearing the air raid sirens wailing, and then being made to hurry downstairs where the whole family was ensconced in our Morrison shelter, a large reinforced steel table that was supposed to bear the weight of the house if it was bombed. It was great fun and we became rather blasé after surviving several air raids without incident, but in the end we were caught out.

One night I awoke to the sound of a low-flying aircraft overhead, followed by a gigantic explosion. Then the house fell apart around me. I was covered in dust and huge lumps of plaster and I remember looking up to see stars where the ceiling used to be. We were later told that one of our bombers returning from an aborted raid on Germany was badly damaged and had jettisoned its bombs, the pilot mistakenly thinking he was still over the North Sea. A little shell-shocked, I lay there for some time before my uncle appeared out of the dusty gloom and carried me down what was left of the stairs.

I was deliriously happy to find that all my family had survived with only minor cuts and bruises and I enthusiastically hugged them all with huge relief. During the summer holidays, double summertime meant it stayed light until almost midnight and we were often allowed out late to watch formation after formation of Lancaster bombers passing over on their way to bomb Germany. We kids cheered and waved our Union Jacks like crazy, believing, as children do, that they could see us too; and I recall my grandmother wiping tears from her eyes and saying, 'God Bless our boys and bring them home safely.'

One Sunday afternoon there was more drama. Like many young lads at that time I was a wizard at identifying aircraft and my friends and I were playing in the field next to our house when I saw a low-flying RAF Westland Lysander appear over the rooftops, a few hundred yards away. We were fascinated as we had not seen one so close before, and we all ran home immediately to tell our folks. It proved to be a life-saving move as the Lysander circled round one of the houses several times before coming in too low and catching one of its wheels on the chimney stack. It cartwheeled a few times before crashing into the field where we had been a few moments before, and broke up with a huge explosion. We were horrified at the disaster and white-faced at our narrow escape. My grandfather, who every weekend was a member of Scarborough's 'Dad's Army' or the Home Guard, as it was known then, was first to the crash but could not get near enough because of the heat.

Sadly, it seemed both members of the crew had died instantly. It unfolded later that the pilot had been circling round his mother's house and waving to her prior to making his tragic mistake.

Considering that I had been evacuated to somewhere that was supposed to be safer, I was having a particularly exciting time, but I loved every minute of it. I remember looking out of my bedroom window one evening and seeing a twin-engine aircraft fly past with German markings on it. It was quite close and very low and I immediately identified it as a Junkers 88.

I ran downstairs frantically shouting, 'There's a German plane just flown past but the air raid siren hasn't gone.'

I could not understand why none of my family believed me and I distinctly remember my grandmother laughing at me until I rushed outside and showed them, by which time it had climbed higher and was beginning to turn into a dive towards Scarborough harbour where there was a Navy minesweeper docked.

It released a stick of bombs, which we learned later had totally missed their intended target, and then it started to climb up and away over the sea. That was not the end of the drama as two RAF Spitfires appeared from nowhere and gave chase. I rushed up to my bedroom for a better view and saw the end of the Junkers as it was caught and shot down over the North Sea. I had no idea what was going on in Hull but I sure was witnessing my share of the war here in Scarborough.

I mentioned that my grandfather was in the Home Guard and he became a bit of a legend for being the only member of his troop to fire a shot in anger at the 'enemy'. He was on duty down at the guard post on the seafront one evening when another of our Lancaster bombers was returning from Germany in real trouble with two engines damaged and bits missing everywhere. You would think things could not get any worse for the over-stressed crew but it sure might have done. My dear old grandfather was not strong on aircraft identification and, when he was on duty, any aircraft low enough was an enemy and fair game.

He promptly raised his ancient Lee Enfield rifle and loosed a wild volley of shots at the hapless Lancaster. Fortunately, it was well out of range and granddad was no Buffalo Bill, so no-one was any the worse for the encounter. He never lived down that episode.

Several times in the early part of the war the Luftwaffe subjected Scarborough to night attacks with incendiary bombs and parachute mines. Sometimes they also dropped parachute flares first that lit up the ground so they could see where to drop their explosives. We could hear the incendiaries raining down on the town and the sound was like marbles dropping on a hard floor. The resulting fires lit up the night sky and we feared that the whole town would be destroyed; but it turned out that they did not do as much damage as expected, thanks to the heroic efforts of our firemen and an army of volunteers. My grandfather brought one of the expired bombs home one day to show us but my grandmother told him to throw it away - but I know he kept it in his garden shed until after the war.

In September 1943 I returned to live with my recently-divorced mother in our native Hull to attend the grammar school where my grandfather taught. Despite the severe damage inflicted on the city by the blitz, the house where my mother lived was relatively unscathed.

Explosions a few streets away had loosened plaster, rattled windows and scared her witless – but she survived.

Now it was Germany's latest terror weapon, the V-Bombs, also known as Doodlebugs, that we had to look out for.

I remember shivering with trepidation almost every night it seemed, as we heard them chugging overhead and waited for the noise to stop, signifying the end of its journey and its plunge to earth before exploding. Cycling to school the morning after a Doodlebug raid was always a different and exciting challenge. Life was tough for everyone but I remember being very content, even happy, as I began to feel that I might actually survive the war. I spent a lot of time on my own so I certainly had to grow up quickly and I learnt some valuable lessons about life. My mother worked shifts as a telephonist and I had to cope with school work and look after household chores as well as do all the shopping. Who says men cannot multi-task?

At my grammar school I discovered that all the young teachers had gone off to serve in the armed forces when war broke out and we had a collection of grizzled old-timers to manage our education. Not all of them appeared to be thrilled at being dragged out of retirement and these grumpy old dinosaurs frequently took their bitterness out on the pupils. We got a reality check after the war when gradually the old guard returned to retirement and a succession of enthusiastic young men took their places, happy to have survived the war.

The biggest blow of all was the arrival, in September 1946, of a super-fit young Adonis who was to be our physical education teacher. Until that time we had become soft and lazy under the guidance of an ancient, arthritic, ex-WWI veteran, who struggled to walk, never mind teach, and we grew steadily more disillusioned and unruly; I suspect we made the dear old man's life a misery.

At first it was a painful transition for us. We learned that Adonis had been a commando in the early part of the war and had then become an instructor at a paratrooper regiment training camp somewhere in Herefordshire. He had trouble at first in realising that we were kids and put us through a gruelling series of fitness routines that nearly killed us. His first act was to prepare a punishing cross-country course which we were expected to tackle at least once a week, each one a Herculean task for our untrained and sometimes under-nourished bodies. He eventually learned to tone down his efforts to turn us into Olympic athletes after a few parents of the more sickly boys came to complain; and as time went by he almost managed to get down to our level.

In retrospect, I give him full credit for awakening my interest in sport, particularly athletics and football. However, the one black spot in what was often an enjoyable, if sometimes painful, induction into the joys of participating in sport was 'The Wet Games Afternoon'. I blame this phenomenon for the two opposing effects which it had on me in the following years: it gave me a jaundiced view of dancing, which stayed with me for many years, and it aroused my hitherto dormant interest in the opposite sex. Happily, I no longer hate dancing and have even taken part in a coronary-inducing céilidh or two. As for the ladies, I can say that my interest in the fairer sex has never waned.

Games afternoons were always on a Friday and most of us looked forward to them because there were now a lot of exciting new skills to learn, and chances to play in the newly formed school football, cricket and athletics teams. However, there was a downside to it occasioned by our English weather. If there was the slightest drizzle or the sight of a black cloud it was enough to convince our newly-caring games master that getting wet would be severely detrimental to the health of his dear pupils. However, in order for Adonis, as we now nicknamed him, to maintain his macho image he would always stress that he personally didn't mind the rain as he played rugby every week in monsoon conditions; but he jolly well wasn't going to force us to do the same, thus cleverly putting the responsibility on us and making us feel like wimps.

A clear majority of the boys, knowing what the alternative was going to be, would happily have opted for the monsoon every time. I suspected that Adonis looked forward to these sessions as the very sporty and attractive blonde girls' games mistress, a sort of Betty Grable look-alike, was always there to chaperone the girls, assist in the torture, and operate the gramophone. Needless to say, rumours about the pair later became rife, especially when a boy found them kissing behind the curtain in the school hall and couldn't wait to spread the news; the lady left suddenly at the end of term and was never seen again.

On such Fridays, when all our prayers had failed miserably and it was raining enough to persuade Noah to build another ark, around one hundred of us fifteen-year-olds, roughly an equal number of boys and girls, were shepherded into the dimly-lit sports hall where we immediately gravitated to same-sex sides of the room as if by some giant automatic sorting machine. Although it was a co-educational school, the two sexes were usually kept apart until they entered the Holy Grail of the sixth form. Wet games afternoons were the only occasions when fraternisation on a limited scale was allowed in school.

The girls occupied one half of the sprawling two-storey building and had their own headmistress, a formidable spinster in her fifties, who ruled her domain with a rod of iron and had an inherent dislike and mistrust of the male species. We, and seemingly most of the staff, were terrified of her. To see her marching into our half of the school on one of her rare visits, swishing her obligatory cane and scowling ominously at any of the male species that got in her way, could not have had more impact if it had been Adolf Hitler himself.

There we stood, facing the 'enemy' like opposing armies on a battlefield, attempting to look nonchalant but barely concealing our embarrassment. Before the first of these terpsichorean disasters a small number of misguided souls amongst us boys seemed to be experiencing a flutter of excitement at the prospect of dancing with a girl, but this soon vanished when the reality struck home. After all, this was 1947 in post-war Britain and fifteen-year-old boys at that time were as different from their modern day equivalent as Desperate Dan is to Hugh Grant.

Our apparent objective, once we had been browbeaten into accepting a girl for a partner, was to learn how to dance the Sir Roger de Coverley, a complicated sort of barn dance. Adonis never worked out that if the girls had been asked to do the choosing instead it would have gone much more smoothly as they were, I recall, so much more mature than us and were definitely more up for it than we were. It is embarrassing to look back and remember how utterly unready we were for this and how crassly we behaved in the early stages of these confrontations - me included, unfortunately.

No matter, by the time the ensuing turmoil was sorted out there was usually only half an hour left to continue with the dance training. Sorry to say, that by the third wet Friday of the autumn term and our third attempt at mastering 'The Roj' (as it became known) we were still as uncoordinated and clueless as the first time, and any glimmer of interest we once had was waning rapidly.

Mainly due to lack of space and exacerbated by a lethally slippery floor, collisions were legion. Some were accidental, but I suspect that many were deliberately engineered. Nowadays, the Health and Safety police would have had a field day. Finally, an increasingly frustrated and angry Adonis would have to wade into the carnage like a rugby referee sorting out a brawling scrum.

By the end of the afternoon his bonhomie began to evaporate and Dr. Jekyll inevitably became Mr. Hyde. We had to admire him though. Like us he was well out of his comfort zone but he never gave up. I think eventually he began to pray for fine weather every Friday.

Years later, after service in the RAF followed by university, I became a teacher myself and experienced the other side of the coin. Looking back, I now feel much more kindly towards Adonis. He had taken on a difficult job and his commitment and enthusiasm could not be questioned. We must have driven him to drink. However, the legacy that I inherited from those early days, a first-hand understanding of the futility and waste of war, and a passionate love of all sports, has stayed with me all my life. Throughout my thirty-two year career I always tried to pass on to my pupils the same feelings, the same enthusiasm and dedication that I felt. I like to think that most times I succeeded.

- 5 -

Mistaken Identity

This story took place when I was growing up in the countryside on the Essex/Suffolk border, back in the late 1970s and early 80s. As those of my age may also recall, I have memories of hot summers, seemingly endless holidays (although school summer was only six weeks) and a very limited ability to distinguish much between one year and any other.

One activity that was frequently undertaken during these summers (at least by my family) was 'strawberry picking' – or sometimes more generically 'berry picking'. For those unfamiliar with this pastime – as it seems to be less widespread nowadays – it was basically an open air, giant 'pick and mix' but with fruit and not sweets.

One would go to a venue (normally a farm or significantly sized field) where land had been set aside to grow row upon row of strawberries, raspberries, blackberries, etc.

In an era well before CCTV on every street corner, chip-and-pin codes and identity cards, people would simply turn-up at these farms with whatever they thought was a suitable container, pick the fruit of their choice, take the crop to a weighing station and pay (cash, of course), before driving home. There was no limit to the amount of time spent selecting one's berries, nor was there anyone checking how much fruit any individual decided to eat (as opposed to being put in their container).

Anyway, on one particular excursion my mother and father, together with my brother and I (aged around 7 and 9) went to the next village to get the ingredients for pudding that evening.

One of the farms there had a large, multiple berry selection to choose from, and so we drove in and scattered into the warm summer sun. As per normal, we each took a pot and went our different ways to pick or eat whatever took our fancy (or just to play in the sun once we had become bored with that).

After a couple of hours my parents had purchased a suitable selection of fruits and were ready to go home. However, the field was quite large, and the hedges relatively tall, so that after about 15 minutes of looking for us, they were still walking around with some pots of increasingly warm berries and still lacking two energetic boys.

They decided to go to the 'check-out area' (which was nothing more than a folding table dragged outside from the owner's house, a set of scales and plastic tub with coins and notes) and ask for help. My mother approached the lady serving and the conversation went as follows.

'Excuse me, but we are looking for our two sons. They were around here somewhere, picking berries. Have they come to you or have you seen them at all?'

'I am not sure – where did you see them last?' replied the woman.

'They were over in the loganberries,' said my mother.

'And what do they look like?'

'Well, they are a bit like gooseberries; only longer.'

Not surprisingly this did not help the search, and although my mother corrected herself, what was done, was done, much to the amusement of my father as well as the lady serving.

- 6 -

A Marriage Proposal

We all have grand plans, right? I don't mean in a Miss World, end poverty and famine sense. I just mean the big things in our own lives. You know, kids, new job, moving house, that kind of thing. Of course, we might have more chance of ending world famine single-handed than actually affecting anything in our own lives.

Take my friends Bob and Lydia, for example. They had been trying for a baby for like five years or so. Two Christmases ago, at one of our college friends' reunion dinners, Bob announces to the room that they have now stopped trying and have accepted that they will remain forever childless. Of course, Lydia burst into floods of tears and one of the lads cracked a joke at Bob's expense in an attempt to lighten the mood but the whole thing was a bit of a downer.

By Easter, they were expecting!? Turned out to be twin girls, absolutely gorgeous – perfect, healthy bundles of joy. Here we are, not eighteen months later and Bob and Lydia have separated and are getting a divorce. He's shacked up with his secretary and Lydia and her girls could not be happier.

It seems they just had to work through their own personal struggle together and then they were always destined to go their separate ways. The 'pregnancy gods' were against them right up until the final whistle. Then, just as they prepared to accept defeat and whilst the gods were asleep at the back, Bob scored during time added-on although now, of course, he is playing away!

That is just one example. No doubt there are dozens that each of us can recollect where a simple plan falls down on execution or conversely, human spirit triumphs against all the odds. Well here is mine and it is all true.

My grand plan was my marriage proposal to my wonderful wife. Without wishing to give away the ending, she is now my wife and therefore despite everything you are about to read, 'the boy done good', as they say.

Everything was starting to go so well for us both. I had just changed jobs for more money which meant we had been able to put down the deposit and just about afford the mortgage repayments on our first house. Money was tight though but I reckoned I could juggle a few things such as put the gas cheque in with the electric bill and vice versa to buy a little time. On that basis, I was just about able to afford the engagement ring and my reason for choosing 'that ring' over any other, was the free Airmiles that came with it.

Go back 12 months and my girlfriend and I went on our first date on a sunny August bank holiday weekend. My grand plan was taking shape nicely and would involve champagne and one knee at the top of the Eiffel Tower in Paris, on the bank holiday weekend just one year later. Incidentally, August bank holiday became our 'thing' and we were also married on that same weekend two years later but I digress.

One of the national newspapers had been running a clip-and-collect token promotion for a two night stay in Paris. It was not the Meurice obviously but there was a list of a dozen decent(ish) hotels you could stay at and I had duly clipped and collected my 30 tokens or whatever it was and the booking had been made.

I now had the newspaper tokens and enough Airmiles for two flights from Heathrow to Paris and booked the flights leaving mid-afternoon Saturday of the bank holiday weekend. We would be strolling along the Champs-Élysées by teatime. What could possibly go wrong?

My wife sometimes calls me 'last minute Lil'. I am sure I am not the only man who works too hard, makes lists and achieves everything that needs to be done, just in the nick of time. The same was true of our weekend in Paris. I finished work on the Friday night, we had a takeaway and watched some nonsense on the TV. Next morning would be easy-peasy: chuck a few clothes in the case, grab the ring and the passports, and make sure we are away by 9 am. Only, I couldn't find my passport!

I knew I that had one and I knew for certain that I had seen it recently, but I couldn't for the life of me remember why or where. We turned the house upside down and I phoned the embassy and was told quite clearly: 'No passport, no Paris!'

But that can't be right surely, we're in the bloody EU. How hard can it be? I only want to pop across the Channel and pop the question.

We live in Yorkshire and Heathrow is about 200 miles away. But I had been planning to make the drive anyway, so why not chance it? We drove all the way and four hours later spoke to a very sympathetic lady on the check-in desk, who called her less than sympathetic boss over. Words were exchanged and possibly a few insults and then the police were called.

Fortunately, they saw the situation for what it was: a desperate young man trying to do the right thing. As it turned out the right thing was for me to give up on Paris, my tokens and my Airmiles, in order to not get arrested.

I have never been a defeatist. These things are meant to be and anyway who cares about smelly old Paris when we have wonderful London on our doorstep.

We high-tailed it into the West End and en route, I refocused my grand plan – posh restaurant, take in a show and book a hotel nearby. The credit card would take a bashing and I would have to juggle a few more utility bill payments but that would beat Paris and the Eiffel Tower any day.

Now I don't know London very well, being a Yorkshire Lad and all, but I was not afraid to drive on the busy West End streets and I was sure we would figure it all out as we went along. All I really needed to do was dip in to one of those kiosks, choose a show for tonight and then find somewhere to eat. I even managed to find somewhere to park, which was a stroke of luck in itself and we wandered into Leicester Square. By now it was evening and there were not too many choices of show for tonight's performance.

We settled on *The Bible: The Complete Word of God* (abridged) by The Reduced Shakespeare Company – I kid you not and it was not at all bad but we are getting ahead of ourselves.

First we needed food and we found a lovely little Italian restaurant. It was packed, which I took to be a good sign, and the waiter stuck us on the end of another couple's table. We ordered a nice bottle of wine and, given that we were now on a bit of schedule, we also quickly ordered our food. After 90 minutes and with no sign of our meals, I had my second heated exchange of views that day and we left. A quick dip into MacDonald's and we just about made our seats in time for the performance. It was then that I remembered the hotel or rather I remembered that I had forgotten to book one.

As I said already, the show was good but my heart was never quite in it. I knew that we would have had slim chance of happening upon a hotel with a vacant room on any Saturday night in London, let alone August bank holiday weekend. There would be no other choice than to drive the four hours home again.

Unfortunately, that was not to be the last of my disappointments for the day. Upon returning to the car, it transpired that I had not properly read the sign and had been parked in a permit holders' only bay for the last five hours. Needless to say there was a penalty notice stuck to my windscreen. As we set off back to Yorkshire, I just wanted that day to be over but the fates were not done with me yet.

I would bet I was still inside the North Circular when I first got flashed by the speed camera. I remembered reading somewhere that you could not get more than one speeding fine on the same day as theoretically you could lose your driver's licence before you got back home.

Despite not having any relevant qualification, I decided that must be good law and put my foot down! It was probably 3 am when we finally arrived home and I have to admit that I felt a little beaten.

Sunday then, and I woke with renewed vigour and a revised plan. Who needs Paris or even London? We live in Yorkshire for goodness sake - God's country. Everyone claims that of course but we have the Dales on our doorstep. Plans do not get much grander than one (damp) knee and a shouted marriage proposal over the roar of the Gunnerside Gill. We showered, breakfasted and then a quick jaunt up the A1 and we were in Leyburn. The sun was shining, I had the ring and being a Yorkshire Lad, this time I didn't need a passport.

Until that very day, I had never before heard of The Sealed Knot. It turns out that they are the oldest battle re-enactment society in Britain and the largest in all of Europe, whose members number several thousand. And on that glorious bank holiday weekend every single one of them had descended on the Yorkshire Dales. They had apparently travelled from every corner of Britain to 'pretend' that they were fighting in the English Civil War and they had all brought their families along for the weekend.

Needless to say, there was not a room to be found in a hotel, guest house or outhouse within a 50 mile radius. Thwarted yet again, I would at that point have taken on every last one of them in hand-to-hand combat. There was to be no marriage proposal high on a hill in the Dales this day. Was this a message that I was being sent so unsubtly? Am I not destined to marry this girl, will she leave me for another or is she just after my money, which was dwindling fast?

I knew it could not be any of those things of course and I saw The Sealed Knot for what it truly was - a test of our love. I would have to think again but I would not be found wanting!

About six miles from where we lived, was a wonderful Spanish restaurant. At least I had heard rave reviews and I knew that the setting was beautiful in an old windmill but sadly we church mice had not so far been able to afford a visit. But this was different, this was life changing, this was my further revised grand plan. If we could not go to Paris, London or the Dales then we would bring a little bit of Spain to us.

I can still remember stopping at the phone box and working through a mental checklist so that nothing would be left to chance. Yes, they had a table for two at 8 pm and, yes, they would put the champagne on ice. I even remembered the taxi, which would pick us up at 7.30 pm. We had loads of time to get back home, shower and change and be picked up and whisked off for *una estupenda velada romántica*.

This would be it, a great meal, a bottle of fizz and given that she might not appreciate being the centre of attention in a small restaurant, I would pop the question in private after we got home.

And that is how it went, up to a point. The restaurant was everything I had heard it would be, the bill was even more than that but the wine had been full bodied, the champagne cold and good quality and spirits were high. At long last and about time, the pieces were falling into place. All that was left was to arrange a cab home and do the deed.

There are moments in life when people will say 'I didn't know whether to laugh or cry'. This sorry tale of bank holiday weekend misery was crying out for a final punchline and so it came, as the waiter returned with the message that he had tried every taxi company in town, all of which were fully booked. The earliest cab would be 10 am the next morning – well it is bank holiday Monday!

That is the point when you start looking around for the cameras, thinking who has set me up and why did I not spot it earlier in this fiasco. Any minute my best mate would come round the corner arm-in-arm with Jeremy Beadle, waving my passport in his hand. But no, the look on the waiter's face confirmed that he was deadly serious and more than that, he was now genuinely worried for us.

'How far have you got to go?' he asked.

'Oh about six miles, just the other side of town!'

After everything we have eaten and drank tonight it would take us longer to walk home, than it had done to drive up from London. Good grief, was that only last night?

We began to laugh of course, that hysterical hollow-eyed laughter, which can go either way. The restaurant staff huddled together for a brief moment and then the owner wandered across. I was not sure what was coming next, had my credit card bounced? Nothing would have surprised me. And then as a true Samaritan she explained that one of her staff lived not far from us and had said that he would be willing to drive us home. Thank you Enrique.

Of course, we would have to wait until he finished his shift at one in the morning, but still...

And there we have it, a grand plan that went to pieces. At least my proposal of marriage to my wife was more memorable than yours. I asked her over tea and toast in bed on August bank holiday Monday, 1997, and we finally tied the knot (or should that be sealed the knot) August bank holiday two years later.

We have three lovely children, none of whom were born on a bank holiday weekend and I have every intention of never letting go of any of them and certainly not my wonderful wife. I am never going through hell like that again!

And my passport? Well, do you remember that new job I had just started? Turns out I had taken my passport in to the office on my first day as the HR department needed to keep a copy on my file. I found it in my desk drawer the following week. I told you I had seen it recently.

- 7 -

The Proposal

He emerged on the street from the steps of the comfortable belle epoch Hotel Lutetia into the bright sunshine of a spring day in Paris. He checked his pockets: photograph, map, two packs of Gitanes Sans Filtre, lighter and sufficient Euros. Oh, how he mourned the demise of the familiar Franc and still occasionally he made mistakes by a factor of ten or so, when on a spree.

He took a moment to orientate himself with the map, light a Gitane and reassure himself that this would be a most special day. He set forth with measured purpose, the heavy black hobnail boots making a satisfying 'clack' on the granite kerbs and stone flags as he went.

He was quite tall, but not as tall as he once was, and heavily built, a cross between pit prop and barrel. He wore a heavy black canvas bib and brace, and thick checked shirt and aged Breton beret, flattened to the shaven head on both sides, in the traditional style. The only other adornment was the broad black leather belt which gave a hint of definition between waist and chest. Similar to *Shrek*.

It was an imposing enough sight to ensure that he rarely had to 'give way' to oncoming pedestrians or even the Parisienne traffic as he undertook his mission.

He arrived at the first location marked on the map. Fnac, on Rue Des Rennes to collect the pre-ordered DVD of Marcel Carne's classic *Le Jour se Lève*, the noir story of a gangster, doomed to die in an armed siege, having lost his only true love.

At the second cross, a traditional fine wine establishment, he purchased a bottle of Pol Roget Winston Churchill champagne and paid the extra to have it gift wrapped.

The final destination was different. The first two he knew so well and also precisely what he had wanted: the last he knew not at all. He would need to use his intuition. He decided to rest and gather his thoughts. He sat outside an unassuming back street café and ordered a Pastis and a double espresso. Lighting another Gitane, he gazed at his old black and white photo, as he had done often over the last twenty-five years and savoured the Pastis and coffee.

She was sat astride a wrought iron chair in the Tuileries, hands atop the back of the chair with her chin resting on her hands, designer sunglasses hid her eyes but a beguiling smile spoke for them. She looked insanely happy.

He was reassured, he crossed the street and entered Chantel Thomass, in similar fashion to John Wayne entering a saloon. But this was the finest lingerie shop in Paris. The mademoiselles ceased to browse and chatter and gazed open mouthed towards the door. Stunned silence. Was he a delivery driver or street beggar? A young, tall, impossibly slim and beautiful shop assistant noticed his blustering nervousness and came swiftly over to enquire.

Almost in a whisper he explained what he wished to buy and she understood immediately which lessened his mounting feeling of discomfort. She disappeared and returned carrying several items and took him to a quiet corner of the shop, which had started to resume business as normal. She carefully unwrapped firstly a lacy suspender belt, then the tiniest, finest of thongs and finally some exquisite black silk stockings. All absolutely perfect. She asked the size and he indicated that it was similar to herself. She smiled knowingly . She confirmed that they were extremely expensive. But that was of no consequence.

As she gift wrapped them, he produced the DVD and asked her to place it in the box. Again she smiled and complimented him on his good taste and she remarked that the champagne was perfect too.

'I hope they will do the trick,' he murmured in response.

'Sans doubt,' she replied. 'What woman could resist all this? And you. And in Paris too. Parfait!' There was honesty and conviction in her voice and it made him feel more assured.

It was twenty-five years since they had been in Paris together as carefree twenty-year-olds; and now they were to meet again but with married partners who, in all likely hood, would curtail any romantic notion despite being a thousand miles away and oblivious to the assignation.

The 'clack' of pavement was replaced by the equally satisfying 'crunch' of the gravelly paths of the Tuileries as he passed the Louvre and gazed distantly over toward the Musée D'Orsay, where once they had lunched and become heady with the works of Van Gogh and Monet. He looked over to Angelina's on the Rue De Rivoli, where they had discoursed over the finest *petite madeleines* and coffee and he regarded with slight envy the youth of the city as they frolicked and engaged in the gardens. Would he trade it for the wisdom that came with age? He laughed, 'Wisdom?' But he was not sure that he would not.

As he approached the garden's café, he noted with sadness, and a little anger, that the chairs had been replaced by a more functional modern variant and that most of the tables were occupied; but she was there, seated alone. Even from a distance the world around her seemed to become fuzzy and out of focus. A beacon of style and presence. She was wearing a long black leather coat and black knee-length boots, adorned with silver chains instead of spurs. Her short boyish hair, still immaculately cut, but now with a tinge of grey.

As he neared, she did not seen him approach, her head tilted toward her book but he recognised the grey two-piece suit and familiar black tights. She was always stylish, always perfectly dressed

He placed a gentle hand on her broad shoulder. She knew instantly it was him and she rose from her seat turned toward him and embraced him warmly; they kissed on the cheeks in the time honoured way and she whispered his name in her warm, soft, deep timbre,

'Pongo.'

He struggled to respond but eventually it emerged, 'Perdita.'

They released each other slightly, stared into each other's eyes and smiled. Then they laughed and they held each other for just a little longer than best friends should.

He sat beside her and beckoned the waiter. Perdita recommended the vin rosé and he nodded and then produced his photo and she hers. Very similar but with him on the chair

They talked endlessly, somewhat hesitantly at first but as the wine flowed, and the Gitanes were shared, the trust and chemistry returned and their worlds and words lit up, aligned and were put to right.

It was supposed to end right there. A brief reunion over lunch, for both were in Paris on other missions, with important work to do.

But as their window drew to a close she noted that he'd been shopping.

'Err, yes. Just a little token to mark the occasion,' he confessed.

And he passed the Chantel Thomass bag across the table.

'Mmm... Designer?'

'Mais Oui! Bien sur!'

She unwrapped the champagne and smiled as she recognised the bottle and vintage. She touched his hand and mouthed a 'thank you'. Carefully she started to untie the ribbons of the box and on lifting the lid, espied the DVD and gave a quizzical look.

'There's more.' He motioned and she rifled gently through the layers of tissue to reveal the exquisite black lingerie, she looked up with tears forming in the most beautiful eyes he had ever seen and she kissed him gently but fully on the lips.

There were tears in his eyes too as he rested his head against her breast and placed a hand on her knee.

'Oh Pongo! My Pongo You know it can never be.'

'Aye Lass. That's what you've always told me.'

He sat up straight and then stood beside her caressing her hair as she lay her head against the black belt.

'It's just a proposal. I promised you we would see this film together and tonight we could. I have a table booked at Les Deux Magots for 8.00 pm and a screen in the Lutetia penthouse. May be you could just give it a try? Diner à Deux?'

He kissed her forehead and whispered in her ear that he had to go now and would see her later if she wished. And then swiftly turned on his heels and marched away without looking back for if he did, he knew he would want to stay… forever.

Perdita gently fingered the lingerie and with tears rolling down her cheeks watched the bear of a man she had known for over thirty years disappear into the crowd.

Could it be that she would be at Les Deux Magots once more, after all this time?

- 8 -

The Angel of Death

While people have different interpretations of what life is and how to view it, then come with me as I share an experience that occurred to my brother-in-law in Nigeria.

This particular Sunday in December 2001 dawned as a lovely day in Kano, Nigeria, where he lives. The cool morning breeze, the rosy pale hue of the sunrise, the chirping of the birds in his compound, the doves crooning in their artistically carved dwelling places, all provided a perfect setting to start the day with prayer and thanksgiving to God. This was the day he had been looking forward to for some time.

He was excited as, after weeks of careful planning, the day had arrived for his trip by road from Kano to Abuja, the Federal capital city of Nigeria, which was a five to six hour journey. The excitement was compounded with the fact, that the company he works for, was to close for the annual holidays for one month over Christmas and the New Year.

With his wife on a visit to his three children in New Zealand, he decided that, rather than staying back in Nigeria over the holidays, he would come to the UK to spend some time with me. He therefore had to go to Abuja to obtain the necessary visa for travel to the UK. He was accompanied by a lady director of an Indian company who had come to Nigeria to explore possibilities of joint ventures there.

In Nigeria the most reliable car is the Peugeot 504. Rugged and easy to maintain, it is the average Nigerian's Rolls Royce. Even though this model has long since ceased to be produced in Nigeria, because of it's easy maintenance by any roadside self-styled mechanic, it continues to be the most popular car.

His younger brother working in the same town had a well-maintained such car and he felt that it was safe to travel the few hundred miles in it. Additionally his driver Yakubu, an elderly man, who resembled 'old man Mozz' of the phantom stories, was a very trusted and careful driver. When he drove his eyes would be glued to the road ahead of him and he would be oblivious to anything happening around him.

Thus in holiday mood, the trip commenced after a sincere word of prayer, committing the trip to the Lord. As they had the whole day ahead of them to drive the 500 miles they were not in any hurry to get to their destination. He had a great feeling that all was well on earth and a thrill to be alive.

His lady fellow passenger was seated behind and was full of questions of life in Nigeria and its potential for Indian handicrafts which she dealt in. Their conversations moved from topic to topic and covered various subjects including cultures, the development potentials in Nigeria and the challenges they posed. The scenery en-route was beyond description - from savannah grasslands, to dry arid plains, dotted with hills and valleys, streams and hamlets.

The highway was marked with faded milestones, potholes, carefully and irregularly located. This helped to keep one awake, as you would never know when the car would hit one of these potholes, hear the loud thud, and find the car rise above the ground and then hit back to Mama earth with such force. Never a comfortable feeling.

With the seatbelt holding him firmly to his seat, he was drifting in and out of the land of nod, when all of a sudden, he felt the car surge and become wobbly. Looking out of the closed window, he saw a tyre roll alongside the car. For a flash he wondered the fate of the bloke who lost this tyre.

He then felt his car swerving and heard Yakubu say 'Master, the motor have problems...' And before he could complete his pidgin English, the car that was moving at 110 kms per hour veered off the highway with the driver unable to control it.

In no time the car hit something on the highway, rose over three feet off the road and somersaulted. Suddenly, their heads were on the roof of the car, and they could hear the scraping of the metal roof top of the car on the tarmac. The car seemed to gather momentum, then turned on its side and went into a spin and almost immediately landed right side up.

He heard himself say 'Jesus, Jesus thank you....' But before he could say another word, the car decided to do the same sequence of scrapping its roof on the road, go for a second side spin like a top.

When that happened he heard himself say, 'This joke is going too far...' And then for the second time the car righted itself. Before he could complete saying 'Thank you, Lord', the whole sequence occurred again and he then said, 'Lord, I commit my spirit into your hands...'

Though the car had righted itself, it had sort of flattened: the roof had caved in and the windscreen was in smithereens. It had come to a standstill in a ditch some 20 feet from the highway and about 12 feet below the road level.

He found himself unstrapped from his seatbelt, the car door wide open and lying on the ground like a rag doll. What followed he thinks was a few seconds of total darkness. When he opened his eyes, his mouth had a fair amount of sand and dry grass in it. With his back pinned to the hard earth, his eyes gazing heavenward, and the sun mercilessly blazing downwards, slowly and painfully, the truth dawned on him that various parts of his body were in severe pain. He was unable to move his limbs as freely as he desired. As he blinked, he realised that his specs were no longer on his 'once handsome face'.

As he lay wondering what to do, he just thanked God for keeping him alive. And then the one million dollar question popped up - ' Why me Lord, why me? Why pick on poor me? Did I not say a faithful honest prayer before starting on this trip?' Sadly to this day he has not had an answer.

Within a few seconds he heard the sound of Yakubu saying, 'Oh sorry, Master. Sorry'.

He was in a state of shock, his blue uniform dabbed in dirt and with grass and mud all over him. He came to his side and his immediate reaction was to find out the condition of the lady, who was in the back seat of the car. As he called out her name there was silence and he feared the worst had taken place.

She then answered ' I am alive but I fear I have broken my back'. He then wept not knowing whether out of joy because she was alive or out of sadness because of her injury.

Whilst trying to figure out what to do next, he heard myriads of human voices. He saw about a dozen able bodied men coming down from the main road, into the ditch, where they were. They peered into the car and extricated the lady, who by then was howling in agony and carried her gently up to the main road and then they came for him.

Yakubu was directing them and he saw him clutching onto his handbag which contained money meant for the trip and expenses in Abuja and his UK Visa fees. The bag also contained his passport and other official documents. Also in the car were the lady's travel documents, samples of products she had brought from India and her personal belongings. Under Yakubu's watchful eyes, all these were taken out of the car.

When the rescuers gently lifted him he felt his left leg dangling and in unbearable pain. He realised that he had fractured his leg but unsure to what extent. Though his chest was in searing pain, like having been branded with a hot iron, he could still smile at the irony of being alive.

As his rescuers adjusted themselves, he thought for a moment they resembled pall bearers who wanted to let him know how near perfect they were in carrying a body. With military precision they gently bore him up to the main highway and placed him inside a van. No, it was neither a hearse nor an ambulance - just an ordinary jalopy that the average Nigerian use and refer to as ' a bus'.

There were hectic consultations amongst themselves as apparently all of them were 'chiefs' giving orders that none wanted to carry out. He remembers asking them if they were waiting for the Angel of Death to come. They shut up and then asked him where they could take him. Since he did not know where exactly they were, he could only tell them to get them back to Kano. In hindsight he doubted they would have survived that trip in the state they were in.

The driver of that vehicle took command and asked the rest to wait by the road side while he and a couple of his associates took them to the nearest large town with adequate medical facilities which was 100 miles away.

Later, he came to know, that this was a taxi and the helpers were all passengers. But to him, they will always remain etched in his memory as angels of light, sent to them to help them in their hour of need. This was further enhanced when after reaching the hospital they refused any monetary recompense. He is sure they will be richly blessed for their acts of loving kindness to strangers.

To ensure he was alert during the journey he kept talking to Yakubu, but after about half an hour, he suddenly saw bright lights and then found he could not speak. At the same time he found he could not smile and then realised he had developed a stroke.

He did not expect any immediate medical attention at the hospital as it was a Sunday but for some unknown reason, the consultant orthopaedic surgeon was in the casualty, something he was told never occurs in that hospital. He was a very gentle person, with a soft voice and his smile reassured him that the Angel of Death had bypassed him. He pronounced that he had multiple fractures of his leg with a gaping wound, several bruised areas elsewhere and that he had sustained a stroke.

With Yakubu's help the hospital staff were able to contact the director of his company and eventually transferred to the hospital in Kano where there were better facilities for treatment.

The initial plan was to do the surgery under a spinal anaesthesia but he gently reminded them that this was futile as some considered him spineless with decision making. Additionally the orthopaedic surgeon being a family friend was concerned that surgery would shorten his leg to which he remarked, 'Just break the other leg to ensure they are the same length and touch the ground together'. The surgeon just laughed and proceeded with the surgery.

Few could understand his wry sense of humour at times such as this. They could never understand why he would never complain of the immense pain or make efforts to make those visiting him laugh - he wished he knew himself.

For the following five weeks, with a total of ninety-six injections into his posterior and a multitude of well-wishers from in and around his Kano, he slowly recovered having escaped from the cold hands of the ever ready and eager benefactor – the AOD - The Angel of Death.

- 9-

Two Weddings and an Engagement

It was the Easter holidays of 2010. My two nephews were due to get married and my niece to be engaged. The three events were to take place in India. I have a large family and everyone was going to India to see the weddings and the engagement take place. This meant me or my husband had to go. Due to work commitments it had to be me. Three weeks away, a nice break and an opportunity to shop. What could go wrong?

The challenge started when I had to pack my accessories, jewellery, make up and sarees into a 20 kg luggage allowance; not to mention my comfortable clothes, nightwear and wash things on top of that. It was very stressful and, being the perfectionist, I was constantly thinking I had forgotten something. After all, you don't feel very clever when you get halfway across the world and realise you left something at home. I didn't want to forget something that I would kick myself for over the next three weeks.

I was leaving with my niece as she was coming too but not with her family. She stayed at our house that night as she lives all the way in Leeds and we were both ready to go to the airport in the morning. The next morning we grabbed our suitcases (yes I managed to get everything in there) and headed off to Birmingham airport. I was feeling sad and really didn't want to leave. We had spent a few hours in check in and by the time we were on the plane we were tired. There was no TV so I was limited to reading a magazine for two hours and then spent another eight hours looking out the window and, during the changeover, missing home. A sense of relief rushed through me when the pilot said we would be landing in around ten minutes.

When we got off the plane we grabbed our luggage and searched for Jay-J who was to pick us up from the airport. The trip was around two hours and when we finally got to the house (where I would be staying with family, my niece was staying somewhere else but she was with me for now) we were told we were to attend a celebration of a kind of house warming at my brother-in-law's new house. We arrived tired and I felt as though I must look like a zombie. All the while it was absolutely blazing hot. I cannot stress that enough. After what felt like an age I headed to the house for some sleep. I didn't know it yet, but I needed that sleep more than words can explain.

The next day the weddings were to start. We (myself and the others staying at the house, my niece was no longer with me) woke up, showered, and got into our heavy sarees at around seven every day. I was really missing home especially as the electricity kept going off and sometimes there was not enough water to flush the toilet.

Some of us girls went to a beautician to get our hair and makeup done but she did such a bad job we had to go home and redo it ourselves. (I'm pretty sure she had no idea what she was doing.) Now that I think about it, why did I try so hard? It was so hot the makeup would just slide straight down my face.

The wedding was hot and sticky. The main ceremony was uncomfortable and the food at the reception was horrible. The highlight of the wedding was definitely getting to sit in a limousine for the first time but the plastic roses taped to the outside were a bit tacky. I was absolutely shattered by this time but as soon as one wedding finished another began...

After the first wedding the second began, which meant more late nights and early mornings (sigh). After experiencing the first wedding I knew what we were in for and was not very excited. I did my usual morning routine of showering and dressing. I had to get a really early otherwise we got stuck in the traffic of the busy streets of Punjab and the tedious train crossing, at which we always got stuck because of our bad luck. How we got there was a mission on itself. I had to get a lift to my sister-in-law's house and then I had to get a lift to the weddings from there.

The wedding was probably exactly the same as the first one. The ceremony was warm and sticky and then the reception was awful as the food was outside in the baking heat in the lawn right by the flies. How did I not starve to death over there? I went to stay with relatives the night the wedding finished and it was really nice. We had a pizza to eat which was really nice as it prevented me from turning into a skeleton, although I actually lost around half a stone in weight. I got deli belly and had to go to a doctor to get tablets to help even though I had been careful with my food. This just added to my bad experience.

So the next day was my saviour as it was a chance to lie-in and catch up on my oh-so precious sleep. I had managed to squeeze in some shopping during my stay but this was my first real chance to relax. I'd come back from my little stay over there and I was ready to buy my family some souvenirs for my family and a few outfits for myself and my daughter. It was overall a good day as spent some time with my family like two of my nephews. I was missing my kids and husband though. I was especially missing the sweet, cool, crisp weather in England. It was so hot in India I lost a lot of sleep too because of really hot nights so I was constantly tired.

The engagement was a one day event in a hall. The weather was around 40 degrees Celsius and I thought that I was going to die. The only thing that got me through was the thought of going home soon. The food wasn't very nice at all and I once again went home hungry. It wasn't a very long celebration though so I was getting through it fine, well not fine, but you know, I was coping.

A few people were starting to leave India now. We did a bit of shopping but we were ready to leave. I gave some of my luggage to my sister-in-law as he did not have that much. She left the next day. Some of my nephews left India and arrived home safe and sound. A few more people of my family got home as well. Then my sister-in-law's mother tried to leave and she got stuck at Dheli airport. That was when we found out that there had been an eruption. A volcano had erupted creating huge ash clouds making it dangerous for flights. A few of my sister-in-laws and their children were stuck in Europe somewhere and they couldn't leave the airport because they did not have a visa for that country. I was still in India. Stuck. I wasn't going anywhere.

I was stuck in India. I spent the week hoping my flight would go. No one was able to get in touch with the airlines. It seemed that the offices had just closed all together. One day we went into a shop to collect some pre-ordered clothes. A man in the shop said that it would probably be around two weeks before the flights go. I burst out crying in the shop, I didn't care who saw me. All I wanted to do was go home, I wanted my kids, I wanted my fully functional electricity and flushing toilet. I wanted to go HOME.

The part I was really worried about was spending my birthday in India I was hoping I wouldn't and by some miracle the ash would clear and I would hop on a flight and everything would be fine… but it wasn't.

I ended up spending my birthday away from my husband and kids. We went to see the worst film in the world. An Indian comedy that was meant to be funny but really wasn't. The best part of the day was getting a Subway sandwich which was really nice and tasted like home. You may laugh at me for getting so excited about that one sandwich but hey, I'm a 40-year-old and that remains the best sandwich I've ever eaten in my life.

I was really desperate to get home. I listened out for news on the ash cloud almost constantly, I tried to call my family every day. I was crying on and off all week. I wanted to pack up but I wasn't sure when we were leaving.

It was my husband who got in touch with me and emailed me ticket information to leave. I was so happy I cried. I didn't even believe that I was going to leave. After all, I had been there for a month now. The ash cloud had cleared over England and I was ready to come home. I dedicated my last few to packing up my stuff and cleaning out my room. I was so excited to come home.

When getting ready to leave I was sceptical. I was sure our flight would be cancelled or something bad would happen. I'd just spent a month in India after all and luck really wasn't on my side. I needed to be on the plane before I could get excited or happy. Before leaving I had a Subway sandwich to fill my empty stomach, which was a bit angry at that moment as I hadn't fed it any really decent food in a month. I picked off the extra jalapeños and gave them to my niece. It reminded me of home when I can't eat all the bread of my burger so I give it to one of the kids. I knew I was never mind, I would see them soon.

The plane back was just the same. I had Sodoku and a magazine, I had aeroplane food and I had a nap. I cried a bit too. After the changeover I felt that the plane ride was lasting forever but I was happy to be going home so I just sat back and waited.

The pilot told us we would be landing in 15 minutes through the crackly speakers and I heaved a huge sigh of relief. I swear I have never felt relief quite like that. I vowed I would never go to India ever again.

I clutched my now seemingly lighter suitcases and proceeded to walk through the gate. We were in England. It was raining. Ahh! Sweet rain. I will never take you for granted ever again.

My children were waiting for me on that Saturday evening. My husband said they wanted to see my so much he couldn't refuse to take them. I think my daughter cried. I know I cried. It was one of the most scary, tearful, traumatic and certainly hottest experiences of my life. I've lived up to my vow. Three years later and I still never want to go ever again.

- 10 -

The Holiday of a Lifetime

A number of years ago my family and I were eagerly awaiting our holiday of a lifetime to Bali and Java. We had planned this for over a year and had booked via a very reputable and highly recommended company. In preparation for the trip we had bought several books on the area with a view to getting the most from the holiday. All the necessary vaccinations had been given, and with only a few weeks to go, we were all getting very excited.

Our jubilant mood quickly changed as disaster struck. The holiday company informed us that the airline they were using for the trip had had most of its planes grounded due to safety concerns.

A young woman working for the company took pity on us and began desperately trying to arrange an alternative holiday. Daily phone calls ensued and a number of alternatives were proposed and then sadly discounted due to minor problems with internal bookings. In the meantime we had further holiday vaccinations and were eventually covered to travel anywhere in the world.

With barely a week to go we were offered a holiday to Madagascar. The trip was much more expensive than our booked trip but the company graciously offered it to us for the same price. There was, however, one catch: we needed a visa to travel to Madagascar.

We were asked to complete the relevant forms and sent these together with our passports to the Madagascan embassy. Three days later they had still not arrived and all hopes of having any holiday at all evaporated. However, the next day the passports did indeed arrive and the young lady working for the holiday company once again went beyond the call of duty to sort things out for us.

The company paid to have the visa applications hurried through and these were ready the day before we were supposed to travel. The diligent young lady drove to the embassy and collected our passports and visas which she then left at the airport for us. The journey to Gatwick in the early hours of the next morning was filled with a mixture of excitement for our trip but also deep anxiety as to whether our passports and the necessary visas would indeed be waiting for us as promised.

True to her word our passports, visas and tickets were at the airport and we were soon on our way to Madagascar.

After a short stop off in Paris, we arrived at Madagascar's capital airport Antananarivo around midnight. We exchanged a few hundred English pounds for several large bricks of Madagascan notes and were greeted by our amazing guide for the trip, Su Andrew. He introduced us to the driver of our private bus for the holiday and our adventure began.

The first few days were spent in Antananarivo exploring Madagascar's history and culture. Su Andrew told us all about his upbringing as the son of a village religious leader. His enthusiasm for his country was infectious as was his perpetual smile and laughter.

The next stage of our trip took us to Andasibe National Park where we encountered lemurs in the wild for the first time. Approximately 75 percent of all animal species found in Madagascar are found nowhere else on the planet and lemurs are only found on Madagascar. It is also home to more than 300 species of reptiles, over half of which are also found nowhere else.

The highlight of the trip for me was holding the tiny *Brookesia peyrieras* chameleon in the palm of my hand whilst it played dead, opening one eye intermittently to reassess its situation. This chameleon reaches a maximum length of about an inch and is found in the leaf litter of rainforests and dry deciduous forests only in Madagascar. Night time excursions into the national park revealed an amazing variety of reptiles, amphibians and nocturnal lemurs.

We next visited an entirely different area at Tsingy National Park which is famous for its geological formations as well as its wildlife. This area was also much warmer and drier and this was reflected in the flora and fauna. The last part of our holiday took us to Nosy Be which is a popular tourist area of Madagascar as it has beautiful islands and beaches. This was the first time during our trip that we found ourselves back amongst tourists.

Our trip to Madagascar was exciting and awe inspiring and was indeed a holiday of a lifetime, beating our children's previous favourite holiday to Orlando in Florida by a mile. Madagascar is a unique and fascinating place and I hope to return there again someday; I hope that if I do it will not have been spoilt by the inevitable destruction of its natural habitats.

- 11 -

A Birthday Treat

I have the best sister! For my birthday she surprised me with a weekend shopping spree in Madrid for the two of us. As always she had everything meticulously planned from the minute we arrived at Madrid airport and which streets/shopping centres we will be visiting over the following few days.

We were collected at the airport and whisked to the Hotel Hesperia Madrid where we were booked into our 'pink rooms', they are specially designed to appeal to the high-maintenance women and has created these special rooms to cater to a woman's every whim, there are woman-sized robes and slippers, glossy magazines, complimentary toiletries, a proper hair-dryer and different hangers for skirts and blouses at no extra charge.

We quickly unpacked and set off for the shops. We went to Chueca, a trendy bohemian area not far from the centre of town. If you want to find an amazing one-offs from one of the independent designer boutiques, this is the place to go. It is also the place to go for shoes; so many beautiful shoes with stilettos only a supermodel can walk in but I gave a few pairs a go It would have been rude not to!

So, after a couple of hours we went on to Salamanca which is also known as the golden mile. This is the glamorous area where the high-end designer boutiques can be found. We thoroughly enjoyed Calle Serrano, the smartest shopping street in Madrid and is the place to go for shoes handbags and clothes. There is also a mall which has a good selection of boutiques from some of the best Spanish designers.

After another few good hours of shopping we needed a little sustenance and headed off to a fashionable restuarant on Calle Serrano. We were told that this was probably one of the most famous tapas bars in Madrid and the food hasn't really changed since the 1950s. We had *ensalada de bogavante con vinagreta de narania* (lobster salad with orange vinaigrette), *ensalada cesar con langostinos* (king prawn Cesear salad) followed by *capuchino helado sobre brownie con fruta caramelizada* (chocolate brownie with cappuccino ice cream and caramelised fruit) washed down with a few non-alcoholic cocktails.

We decided that we had done enough shopping for the day and sought out a little culture so we headed to the Museum of Costume for a different kind of fashion fix! It is located in a modern building surrounded by beautiful gardens. The museum takes you on a fabulous trip through the history of fashion and costume from ancient times up to present day.

We then headed back to the hotel and had a quiet evening relaxing in the hotel lounge people watching and talking about our day and what was in store for the next.

Our second day was just as good. Our first stop was to a famous cape maker whose clientele list includes many Hollywood stars. It has been said that Picasso was reportedly buried in his cape from the store. The capes are exquisite, I just had to buy a *capita primavera* in a rich burgundy colour, it was so beautiful! Another place we had to experience the beautiful workmanship is Casa de Diego to look at their parasols, umbrellas and fans.

We stopped shopping quite early and went to a hotel spa and had a 'ritual of the Orient' experience which included a body scrub, body wrap and an Oriental Massage.

After a relaxing afternoon we decided to spend the night on the tiles! We'd heard that the beautiful people can be found sipping cocktails at the Glass Bar in Hotel Urban on Carrera de San Jeronimo so we joined them! It was created to be Madrid's only oyster bar. You are surrounded by glass with a fantastic chandelier which we were told had been imported from Morocco. We had a few cocktails and then stopped at the hotel's restaurant, I would go so far as saying it was the best food I have ever tasted.

As this was our last night in Madrid we decided to party for a little longer and went to Pacha which is a converted 1930s Art Deco cinema with several dance floors, bars and some very good looking people and I'm sure we spotted a few famous faces too.

We had a great evening and it was the perfect way to end a fabulous break of pure indulgence!

- 12 -

A Cuban Crisis

Since I moved to London, I have always wanted to make a trip to Cuba, this island has always fascinated me, so much I heard about it and so much I wanted to see it with my eyes.

I am not sure of the real reason, but as a girl in Italy, my parents and their friends would talk about places to visit and 'must do' travels and countries, like Cuba and Brazil, would always be one of their first choices. Is this to do with Italian culture and its love of beautiful women, language, customs and curiosity? Or because they say Italians are similar to these populations? Thus when it came the opportunity to go, I didn't think twice and decided this was the right time and chance for me to finally see this so much talked about island in the Caribbean.

It was a really cold winter in London in 2009 and very unusual. It was the beginning of December on the day that we took the Gatwick Express; the sky was clear blue and the sun was out but it still felt from one moment to another that was going to change. The cold was nearly unbearable and people knew the weather forecast had already announced that snow was on its way.

My friend Rainbow and I were so excited to be able to travel during this time of the year, and even more excited by the fact the whole trip had come to us by surprise as she had been invited to the Habana International Film Festival to present her film. I couldn't believe my luck. Finally I was going to be in Cuba, watching films, meeting people and taking some vacation before Christmas madness, what else could I wish for?

It is on the plane that our adventures began. Not only were with one of the worst airlines I ever travelled (and I have travelled low costs airlines before) but also this was still a ten hour trip and, only when on the plane, did they tell us it hadn't been refilled with food and snacks. Nothing was available apart from rum and cigars! The plane wasn't full and there was a group of young Cubans returning home, partying, who didn't stop singing, laughing and drinking. Anyway there wasn't much choice on the plane, other than drinking.

We arrived exhausted but still excited to be there. Rainbow had visited Havana and travelled around the island before but she also had never attended the film festival, and Havana is well known for still preserving some of the nicest and oldest cinemas in the world. The entire festival occurs in the Hotel Nacional, a beautiful building from 1930 that has been home to some of the greatest people from the art, politics and literary world.

Beautiful gardens overlook the famous Malecon Hotel; halls, lobbies, corridors and rooms which have been conserved up to today even though the building was damaged during the hard times of Gerardo Machado's dictatorship. This is a hotel which is so emblematic of Cubans' hospitality, such an imposing building which represents a piece of incredible architecture in the Vedado neighbourhood, one of the coolest part of Havana.

The festival ran for nearly two weeks and we arrived towards the second part. We were warmly welcomed by so many great people and enjoying the heat of the city, the beautiful pool, the surroundings, and of course the typical food, white rice, black beans and pork without forgetting our regular daily *mojitos* with the unique taste of what they called their *hierba buena* (mint).

The day of the screening we were taken to the cinema for a previewing test. Rainbow and I were impressed and couldn't believe how beautiful this cinema was and really felt like we were living a different era, a period so distant from us. The theatre has nearly 2,000 seats which of course worried my friend enormously. Could they really fill that cinema with an audience that night? Or would the film be shown to an empty house, making the whole experience from surreal to a nightmare and sadness of seeing such a beautiful space empty?

That night, after the screen had gone black and the credits started unfolding, one person, two, three and slowly everyone stood up and clapped. A standing ovation occurred for several minutes. People smiled and cheered as Rainbow went up on stage to thank everyone. The night was a great success and impossible to forget.

While we were staying in Havana we were lucky enough be taken around the city, not only sightseeing but also experiencing a bit of real life with the local people. Attending events, nights of cabarets like Juana Bacallao one of the last cabaret divas who, at the age of 95, still performs every Thursday night at the well-known Gato Tuerto bar. We drank at Hemingway's popular *mojitos* bar and got to know the Cuban art, music and cinema world. Not to forget that we often ate in what they called *paladares*, typical local restaurants that used to be hidden meeting places for locals. They are still run by locals, some of them situated on great locations overlooking the city.

Havana is full of incredible buildings, streets, memories, and one of the only places I think where you feel as time has stopped. Rainbow told me she already felt that many things had changed and in a certain way had improved since the first time she visited the island many years back.

It was fascinating to go inside incredible old stores, a chair on the corner with a till from the 1950s, old pieces of furniture, windows with old style mannequins, glass cabinets showing the few products available in the store.

At the same time now you would see in different areas many more modern shops selling from clothes to food, soaps, perfumes, creams and house cleaning products. Still not as many as you would think but certainly they are there although most of the time if you see someone inside it is certainly not a Cuban but a tourist or expat. Everything is way too expensive for the locals.

Shops, restaurants, bars, taxis all have different prices for foreigners who are not allowed to use the local currency but only the Cuban Convertible Peso or CUC. Nowadays you see Cubans running kiosks where they can sell food and locals using mobile phones. One day I was looking for a pharmacy, I went inside and again it felt surreal. A long wood counter covered with marble, long glass cabinets filled with all sizes of dark bottles with hand written labels, a bookcase on the back wall where sporadically you would notice boxes of medicines, a few more bottles and many empty shelves. All images which makes you feel Havana is still one of the only cities where you believe you are living in the past every day.

Before going back to London we decided we could take a few days out of Havana and enjoying the tranquillity of the Caribbean beaches. My friend didn't want to go to the well-known Varadero, a beautiful white long beach probably two hours' driving, where only tourists were allowed. A place surrounded by all-inclusive hotels, a concept I never could come to, but with one of the most stunning beaches of the island not too far away from the main city.

However, we rented a car and decided to drive to the opposite part of the coast towards Surgidero de Batabano on the Batabanos coast. A place you can hardly find on the map, suggested by Havaneros (the people grown and bred in Havana) and where supposedly no tourists would be staying. It took a while to drive while we looked for the perfect spot to relax for a few days. The roads were in good conditions in certain parts of the island but we missed a few turns and several hours later we finally arrived to our imaginary paradise. It was before sunset and we immediately reached the beach to see what the place was all about. The village is so small to the point that doesn't even feel there is a village, no cosy hotels just one awful all inclusive hotel and several *casas particulares*. These are Cubans' homes that have a special sign outside the doors to let you know they rent rooms and give you food and look after you. This is the Cuban bed and breakfast.

After all those hours of driving we could only laugh and realized we didn't even know ourselves what we were looking for. At that point we realized that the area had not met with our expectations. We drove around but couldn't see anything, not even a small bar but we carried on laughing and enjoying our holiday time in the warm heat of Cuba. After one of the most insignificant and tasteless dinner (I don't think I can even describe the food we were served) we decided to drive back the same night to the previously unwanted Varadero, a place that then seemed to be a real paradise.

After a few more hours of driving we hoped our adventure would turn into real pure beach relaxation with cocktails, swimming in the crystal Caribbean water and walking on pure white sand. The night was long and as we passed another little village, I started feeling tired of driving. Rainbow has poor eyesight at night, so I had no choice, and was dreaming of getting there when the car broke down.

Oh yes, this is true. In the middle of nowhere, no lights in the street, just beautiful fields everywhere and us with our small rented car which was absolutely dead, giving no sign of life at all. We did not laugh at this point and felt exhausted. We had no idea what to do, how to get the car off the pitch black road (most important as no one could see us).

We spotted a family walking along the opposite side. They had a torch to avoid cars, horses and bicycles that were passing by. Luckily I speak fluent Spanish, and when they saw us the helped to move the car off the road. We couldn't be luckier, right?

Their home was nearby and we all pushed and managed to get that rotten car to their place. They were fantastic, warm and friendly, and opened their home to us immediately offering to call the car service. The most extraordinary moment in their home was chatting with them, drinking coffee and listening to their stories. People who have absolutely nothing, earning about ten to fifteen dollars a month if they are lucky, and here they were helping us, making calls, offering coffee. Both my friend and I were fascinated by the fact that although this was a very modest home, it had the biggest TV and speakers system, as tacky as could be, which took half the space in their tiny living room.

Our small nightmare became such a cool and wonderful experience with a Cuban peasant family, something we won't forget. We finally were taken by their car service to Varadero where no hotel available and there were no *casas particulares*, as too late at night to ring the bell. We were two exhausted women who only wanted a bed to sleep. Out of desperation Rainbow managed to convince an old Cuban man, who was sitting outside his home smoking his cigars, to let us staying at his official bed and breakfast. I think we tried to wake up the entire neighbourhood until this man took pity on us.

The next day and half was lovely and we moved to a little hotel by the beach. Varadero had definitively changed; Cubans were allowed to stay and sell fish on the beach and talk to the tourists. I find extraordinary there was a time when you would not see a local doing business with foreigners or even being allowed to be there.

The place turned out to be a beautiful white sandy beach and the water is as you see it on vacation brochures. We enjoyed our time there but by the time we were finally relaxed, we had to drive back to the hotel in Havana where we had left our luggage. We grabbed our heavy film cans, changed into winter clothes and drove back to the airport.

We made it and arrived early morning to find London covered by snow. That made us happy. However, we were shocked by the low temperature and our adventures seemed nothing more than nice memories. We would have rather have been in the sunshine, stranded in the middle of the fields; but that morning it all seemed like just a nice story to remember. We were back to reality but Christmas was at our door and everyone was in full party mood.

- 13 -

A Birthday in Egypt

All the recent upheaval and bad news stories about Egypt have sat very badly with me as I can only recall how fantastic a country and people they are from my visit there some four years ago on a trip that was a treat from my wife for my 40th birthday.

It had been my long time wish to cruise down the Nile so imagine my delight when my wife presented me with just that opportunity. The trip started off with three nights in Cairo followed by seven nights cruising down the Nile. I really hadn't researched my wish previously so just decided to let it pan out without any detailed research whatsoever – just a few basics on Egypt and formalities on travel.

My abiding memory of Cairo was just how alive, chaotic, mad, diverse and just plain unbelievable a city it was. The traffic was complete madness and at any time you encountered a small truck with maybe four camels standing in the back of it where really there was only room for at most two.

Goats, cattle, chickens, pigs – we met them all in the six-a-breast traffic with seemingly not a single traffic law in force and people almost literally travelling by the seat of their pants. It was a real eye opener and I must say an adrenalin rush just to be in the middle of it.

We stayed in a lovely hotel right beside the pyramids – indeed they were just outside our window. Magnificent is the only words that spring to mind. I come from a construction background and to try and understand the practicalities of building one of these enormous structures with modern tools and equipment never mind thousands of years ago was just mind blowing. It was great to stand and watch the various traders and hawkers trying to sell to the public, sometimes in a seemingly aggressive manner but that is just their form.

After two nights in Cairo we boarded our cruise liner. Now having cruised on luxury liners twice previously, I was a bit naïve on what a cruise down the Nile would entail. Our 'liner' consisted of a two deck boat with open top and cabins below. Completely functional and I have to say fantastic.

We met up with people with whom we are still in touch today and spent several lovely evenings aboard our liner just cruising on the Nile. To write this down brings all the memories flooding back like it was yesterday. We had costume nights dressed up in traditional Egyptian dress, karaoke nights and food nights – all brilliant.

Every day we stopped at another fascinating, mind blowing, location; too many and diverse to mention but we hit all the main ones including The Valley of Kings, Valley of Queens, Abu Simble, etc.

We also went on a balloon ride and that was another recent disaster on the news. I'm pretty certain it was the same trip that we went on; an early morning start with the sun rising as the balloon rose into the sky and then a two hour ride to our destination. So there but for the grace of God and all that.

An abiding memory is of our Egyptian host aboard the cruiser whom took a great shine to a young English girl in our group. As I said previously the Egyptians can come across as aggressive and very forward and it is a man's world, so he just couldn't understand why his advances were being rebuffed.

We spent many times laughing at his lack of progress and bemusement with this strong headed English girl whom he believed should have fallen at his feet with his manly charm. Fantastic.

I have watched the news recently and it saddens me greatly to see the upheaval and unrest in Egypt. It's never good in any country but it sits right on my heart to see it happening now. My mother's best friend married an Egyptian Christian and their family have been living under virtual house arrest and fearful for their lives. That has caused my mother great distress. We all hope and pray that Egypt, and other countries throughout the world, can find a path to peace and reconciliation as some other countries have.

- 14 -

Sailing and Ginger Biscuits

I was going to be brave! My husband had completed his RYA Day Skipper theory and undertaken a five day course in competent crewing so that he could be ready to take to the high seas.

'Why don't you have a go?' This was directed to me, many times. I really was unsure because during my childhood our summer holidays to Ireland would mean crossing the Irish Sea from Holyhead to Dublin. The journey would always have me leaving the contents of my stomach overboard.

As an adult I did not fare that much better. During a holiday to Portugal with my husband and children we boarded a coastal day trip. The boat was beautiful, the wood gleamed it was clearly loving cared for.

Bernard, our skipper for the day, was proud of his boat. Bernard had a 'cure' for sea sickness: a bucket of water and a sponge.

I started to feel unwell about an hour into our trip and out came the 'cure'. Bernard proceeded to soak the back of my neck and then TOLD ME I was feeling better. It did have some affect. When the boat stopped for those on board to take advantage of a swim I took the chance. The lovely cool water made me feel wonderful, and left me with a lovely memory.

So here I am, driving to the east coast to join a group for a competent crew weekend course. I felt at ease as soon as I meet Philip, our skipper for the weekend. My fellow crew members were a married couple, Jane and John, and Janet, a retired lady. They all had some previous sailing experience but I was a complete novice. We went below deck to have a cup of tea and learn about the weekend. When I explained to Philip I felt a little queasy he looked shocked and said 'but we are not moving.' He explained he kept a stock of motion sickness pills and ginger biscuits on board. We were shown around the yacht, all 32 feet of it.

My fellow crew members were eagerly explaining their varying degrees of experience. I just said one word: 'none.' However, I was willing to learn and more importantly was able to take instructions whichever way it was given. Philip cooked a light supper, the chatter was each person recalling travel experiences, and the atmosphere was relaxed. I was looking forward to the weekend albeit with some trepidation.

Morning dawned, the weather was noted and our journey planned on the charts. We were on our way; each person was to take a turn at the helm. The water was relatively calm because we were still on the narrow channel from Orford Ness into the North Sea. Over breakfast Philip advised I take some motion sickness pills. I popped two. It was my turn at the helm and all was going to plan; however, I started to feel extremely sleepy. I needed to sit to the side. I had become very drowsy, the pills clearly had an effect on me. Philip suggested a mug of tea and some ginger biscuits, the tea tasted good and as for the ginger biscuits they brought me to life.

We continued our sailing soon we came to open water, the coastline was visible and the wind sufficient that we did not need the engine running. The sails were at full mast and the yacht ploughed through the waves. Philip gave clear instructions that even a novice like me was able to follow. We were heading for Shotley marina for an overnight stay. We radioed the harbour master to secure a mooring for the night. As we approached the marina the sails were lowered we waited our turn at the 'traffic light' system to gain access to the lock before entering the marina.

The evening was drawing in. Philip took us to the club house for a drink before dinner; he purchased a couple of bottles to take back. The wine went very nicely with the spaghetti bolognese and the good company. The day had been absorbing so sleep came easily.

As a new day dawned the weather was not looking too good. There was some talk of getting back to Orford by road because the weather was not ideal for a crew on training but it was decided we should carry on by sea. Our departure was cleared by the Harbour Master. The immediate area was busy due to large container ships, our yacht seemed like a dot compared to them.

Once we were on the open sea and hogging the coast line the visibility was poor so we were unable to see land. The misty conditions changed to what felt like a moderate gale. Water was coming over the sides, and we all needed to be secured by a safety line. I began to feel unwell; Philip saw this and shouted to get to the other side of the yacht so that I could vomit over the side without me going overboard or perhaps more importantly from Philip's point of view no breakfast landing on his deck. At last we were approaching the narrow channel to take us back to Orford Ness. It felt calmer only for the fact we were not so open to the elements.

We still needed to practise our man overboard routine; this was achieved by throwing a fender overboard to be rescued. Each person took it in turns to stand at the side to keep watch, helm the yacht and circle the 'overboard victim', rescuing from the sea by winching the person to safety.

It certainly felt realistic because the weather was still at this time a strong breeze. We needed to get the sails back in but the wind was such that they were flapping. Jane and I climbed up to the sails to hold them until they were tied. At last we moored. We said our goodbyes; my wobbly sea legs had been swapped for wobbly land legs.

Before I started the drive home I telephoned my husband to tell him of the weekend. He was extremely pleased to hear my voice: not only the fact that I sounded fine but that I had had a good time. He said how proud he was of me, exclaiming 'you have expanded your comfort zone'.

I DID enjoy the sailing and ginger biscuits.

- 15 -

Last Day of Summer

I sit on the plush-cushioned window seat, gently swinging my foot back and forth. The early morning sunlight lands on my wrist, leaving the bracelet from my mum glistening. I pull my eyes away from it and gaze out of the window across luscious green fields, all the way to the coastline. I smile as I see Sadie, my cousin's rogue of a sheep dog, tear out of the hedgerow after a rabbit. This is what summer is to me; endless days spent on the beach or in the woods with my cousin, Ben.

For years I've spent every summer down here in Cornwall with Ben and Aunty Cathy. I can't stand the depressing atmosphere that over comes our house every summer. Where I live, in London, there is nowhere to get away from the tears and the empty smile of my mother. It's best for both of us if I'm away.

Some years ago, my dad and uncle were killed during the 7/7 bombings in London. My Mum refused to move out of London and she was adamant she would overcome the grieving. Of course, she was wrong. Every July, she becomes weary and fragile, like a withering flower. She stops sleeping - sometimes she won't even eat. She has Granny to look after her though, so I know she's being cared for.

There it is again – a knocking at the door.

'Anna, breakfast!' calls Ben from outside of my bedroom. I hear Ben skip down the stairs two at a time. I smile, hop down from the window seat and I dart down the stairs after him.

I enter the kitchen and Aunty Cathy smiles as she hands me a lovingly made packed-lunch for my journey home. I smile back and thank her, but I can't help wondering why Aunty Cathy is so different from my mum. Aunty Cathy recovered so much quicker. Even now, at the age of 42, she still looks as young and beautiful as a rose. My mum, well, she never really recovered.

I sit down and start to neatly butter my toast, making sure I spread it right to the edges.

'You missed a spot,' says Ben grinning. I grin back and pretend to kick him from under the table.

I finish my toast quickly; it is then a joint effort between Ben and I to lug my oversized suitcase down the narrow staircase.

As we load my bags into the car, a lump is growing in my throat. I don't want to leave Cornwall. I'll miss Ben and Aunty Cathy so much. I can already feel that dreaded dull ache returning to my chest. And what about the farm? Ben and I spent nearly every day caring for the sick calves or surfing on the beach with the dogs. We can't do things like that in London. There's no beach and absolutely no green fields to keep farm animals. But it's not just that – to me, everything about Aunty Cathy's little cottage in Cornwall spells home. It's the kind of happy, loving home I know I'll miss when I'm back in London.

We're driving to the train station and I roll my window down, desperate to breath in a few last breaths of fresh air, before I am once again masked in the thick air of London.

We arrive at the train station and I'm feeling just as distraught. Even Aunty Cathy looks to be getting a little teary. She pulls me close and whispers,

'I love you.'

I manage to blink back the tears but I can't find the strength to say something back, so I remain silent. She strokes my hair tentatively as if this is her way of telling me she understands.

The train thunders into the station like wild horses, whipping my hair around my face. Ben lifts my suitcase onto the train with little effort. I smile weakly at him and he hugs me tightly.

'We're going to miss you,' he says with a cheeky grin. There's only a year's gap between Ben and I but I've always been the little one – and he knows how much this annoys me. I laugh and wave as he jumps off the train and onto the platform next to Aunty Cathy. The train slowly rolls out of the station gradually gaining speed. Ben and Aunty Cathy wave, and I wave back - still smiling, even though tears threaten to roll like waves down my cheeks. I'm going to miss them both, of course. But I miss my Mum too and I'll be back to Cornwall next year – maybe going home won't be so bad. There are things I miss about London, it's always swarming with people. I also know that, no matter how many bad memories the city holds, it will always be the place I was born and raised. It will always be a place that I'll miss after a while.

The scenery outside the window rapidly changes from green fields to the industrial city of London.

I step off the train at Paddington Station, now anxious to see my Mum. I see her almost straight away through the sea of people crowding the train station. My stomach flips as I see her smile, I'm definitely glad to be home.

.

- 16 -

Averting a Near Disaster

My son Tom was a very boisterous five-year-old boy, always on the go, running and bouncing around. You couldn't keep him still.

We were in Sweden for Christmas staying with my in-laws. At minus 10 degrees Centigrade it was cold and there was plenty of snow for Tom to play with and enjoy.

On Christmas Eve just before lunch we decided to take him for a walk with a sledge to a local lake, whose name in English translates to 'Bird Lake'. We had been for many walks around this lake over the years, especially before Tom was born and knew it well, or so we thought.

The excitement on Tom's face when we took him to the lake that day was a pleasure to see. There was snow absolutely everywhere and the lake was iced over, which was entirely normal for this time of year. In his small hands Tom had a plastic bag full of bread leftovers for the ducks at the lake. Despite the low temperature they seemed happy and eager to run around after the bread that Tom threw in all directions for them.

By the lake was the usual winter sign, written in Swedish: 'Keep off the ice – Danger!'

There were quite a few people milling around the lake. Despite the cold, it was sunny and bright and we could feel the slight warmth of the sun in our faces. The rest of our bodies were wrapped up in very warm coats and hats.

Tom was fascinated by the scenery. It was his first Christmas in Sweden and he had not seen this much snow before in his short life. We had taken the sledge so he could slide down the hill which led towards to the lake. Happily there was a long rope tied to the sledge so that Tom could not get that far away from us on the sledge as we had control of it at all times. It was at this point that Tom's boisterousness got the better of him. He was quite fast on his little legs when he put his mind to it.

He decided at the top of the hill to suddenly get off the sledge and run away. As he ran past me I was unable to get my fingertips close enough to grab his coat, so he got away from me. To Tom it was a game, but to me there was imminent danger as he was running towards the icy lake down the hill some 100 yards away.

I called out to my wife, but she didn't react quickly enough to appreciate the situation. I thought the few people near the lake would realise what was going on as they saw Tom thundering towards the lake in some sort of slalom-fashion and try to stop him. He was weaving to the left and weaving to the right to avoid anyone stopping him reaching his target. But no one did anything at all. All of us just watched the inevitable play out as if we were in a slow motion movie.

I suddenly began to appreciate the horror of what his intentions were. He wanted to run on to the ice.

I then started to run as fast as I could to get to the edge of the lake, but Tom with his head start out ran me and reached the lake before I or anyone else could stop him. It was futile.

Once he reached the lake he ran straight on to the ice about a yard out from the edge and stood still. His head turned to the left to look at me and at that moment the ice cracked, gave way and he went into the freezing cold water. His brand new coat that my wife and I had bought him before Christmas gave him buoyancy so miraculously his head did not go under the water.

At this very moment I reached the edge of the lake and without thinking put my foot over the edge into the water believing it to be very shallow. I was wrong. I thought I knew the lake, but I didn't. My right hand had already grabbed Tom's coat, but as my left foot thought it was going to touch the shallow lake bed at the edge, it did no such thing. I was in the lake up to my neck, literally.

Somehow I got Tom out very quickly. He was screaming and crying both at the same time. My wife got to him shortly after to console and try to warm him up and a couple of bystanders came over to offer their help seeing all the commotion.

There was one remaining problem, no one was helping me! The cold water took my breath away. It was hard to catch my breath or even speak. Everyone had their backs towards me. No one was coming to help. I had to get myself out of the lake. The edge was slippery due to the ice. My hands were blue and numb.

Somehow after three attempts I pulled myself out the lake. I was wet and freezing as was Tom when we were reunited. We rushed home sodden and frozen to a lovely warm bath.

Tom is now 22-years-old and at University. I still shudder to think what would have happened if the ice on that lake had been thicker that year. He may have been able to run out further…

- 17 -

The Cotton Crop

My late father was born in Memphis, Tennessee, in 1917. In 1921, at the age of four, his mother and father brought him and his four brothers across to Britain where he lived the rest of his life but remained proudly American the whole time.

My grandparents had three more children, this time all girls, and settled in a pleasant village to the south of Manchester. Their eight children all married and produced families and I remember that at Christmas gatherings there could be up to 42 cousins present.

I knew my grandfather had an office in the centre of Manchester and I knew vaguely that he had something to do with cotton and was a member of the Manchester Cotton Exchange. I never found out the exciting story until, as a twenty-first birthday present, my parents paid for me to visit the family in America.

My uncle John, the eldest brother, had returned to America as soon as he was nineteen preferring to live there rather than settle in Britain. I discovered on my travels in the States that I had many relatives in New Orleans and in fact that my grandparents had been born and married in New Orleans and grew up speaking French until they were ten-years-old. The reason for this was of course that Louisiana had originally been a French colony until sold by Napoleon to the United States in 1803. To this day elements of the Louisiana State Code incorporate elements of the Napoleonic Civil Code in their legal system.

Whilst visiting New Orleans I was taken around by my very old great uncle (my grandfather's brother) in his big American car. It was extremely hot and humid in New Orleans but he would insist on driving with the driver's window down on the inside of the car dripping with condensation from the humidity fighting with the air conditioning.

He told me about another great aunt who was extremely eccentric and lived just over the border from Louisiana in a town called Gulfport, Mississippi. Gulfport was on the coast and she was notorious for having sat out a hurricane on the roof of her house despite being advised and entreated by the local police to come down and be taken to a place of safety.

She and my uncle told me the tale of the Cotton Crop for the state of Mississippi for the years 1921 and 1922. Prior to then all cotton had been purchased by brokers who were members of the New Orleans Cotton Exchange. They would buy the cotton in batches from the growers and then sell them on the Cotton Exchange to buyers. The cotton was then sent in batches to places like Manchester where further groups of brokers would bid for them and then sell them to the mills in Lancashire.

My grandfather and a partner conceived of the idea of cutting out not only the New Orleans brokers but also the Manchester Cotton Exchange brokers. They toured the state of Mississippi and agreed prices with the growers for the cotton crop as it grew. This had the distinct advantage for the growers in that they knew before the cotton was grown exactly how much they could expect to receive for their crop. Because there was no brokerage involved with the New Orleans Cotton Exchange my grandfather and his partner were able to offer a better price than the brokers would offer later in the year when the cotton was harvested.

To complete the circuit my grandfather was sent by his partner over to Manchester to agree and arrange the sale of the crop. He did not go to the brokers in the Cotton

Exchange but went touring the mills of Lancashire. By cutting out the brokers in Manchester he was able to offer the mills a cheaper price for the cotton than they would have had to pay bidding for it on the Cotton Exchange. Again they had the advantage of agreeing a price before the cotton arrived so they could forward plan their production and their price for selling the cloth.

Everything was in place for a coup. My grandfather's partner in New Orleans was busy collecting the crop as it was harvested when disaster struck. The brokers on the New Orleans Cotton Exchange were somewhat annoyed to say the least that they were being losing the opportunity of profiting from the purchase and sale of the Mississippi cotton crop. They had political influence. In the Southern United States this was not unusual and the brokers exercised their influence on the governor of Mississippi. The Governor placed an embargo on the crop forbidding my grandfather's partner from moving it over the state line. Everybody assumed that the only place to ship the cotton from was the port of New Orleans and if it couldn't cross over the state line into Louisiana it could not get to New Orleans. They then sat back and waited until my grandfather's partner came begging to let them buy the crop off him.

Grandfather's partner was cannier. He realised that Gulfport Mississippi, which is a very tiny harbour which dries out at low tide, would take a ship large enough to take the whole of the cotton crop. He chartered a ship, sailed it into Gulfport and when it dried out at low tide the cotton was loaded on. At high tide the ship floated off and was sailed across the Atlantic to Liverpool, up the Manchester Ship Canal and into the Manchester docks. It was well and truly on the high seas before the brokers in New Orleans awoke to the fact that the cotton was gone.

Fortunately for my grandfather the worthy brokers of the Manchester Cotton Exchange did not wield any political influence and he was able to unload the crop and deliver it to the mills he had sold it to. Everybody was happy apart from the two sets of cotton brokers and I believe that my grandfather and his partner made a killing. Certainly my grandfather settled in the Manchester area and lived the rest of his life there.

I think however that both my grandfather and his partner felt they had experienced enough excitement for one year and I feel that my grandfather's partner felt that since the political pressure had not succeeded, further more direct pressure might well be exerted if they tried a similar coup in the future.

They both decided to become respectable and my grandfather joined the Manchester Cotton Exchange and his partner joined the New Orleans Cotton Exchange.

They were certainly trading throughout the Second World War and I think my grandfather remained a member of the Manchester Cotton Exchange for some years after that. The Cotton Exchange finally closed in 1968 and the building became a theatre some five years later.

I have tried to find confirmation about the purchase of the Mississippi Cotton Crop of 1921/22 but without much success. The story is told from family memories and other than that I cannot vouch for its veracity.

- 18 -

Would you Believe It?

It was eight years ago that we sold our house. A sad day for me as I particularly loved it, but my wife had no fond memories of it anymore. I was not involved in the meeting of prospective buyers; and nor did I want to be as I was working all hours on my business. I was also abroad a lot, so I left all that to my better half. We moved only a few miles away to a quiet country lane and down-sized to a bungalow. I knew it was the right thing to do and was done so for tragic family reasons.

My wife is not a well lady and does not do holidays but prefers to use her creative side doing pottery and water colours. However, she knows I love anything to do with ships and spotted that the last sea-going paddle-steamer in the world, *The Waverley*, was doing some trips from Glasgow up and down the Clyde.

I used to do these trips as a youngster and she thought it a good idea for me to book a few days away and enjoy myself. I could not say no and so I booked a number of trips on *The Waverley*, a room at a hotel before driving to Glasgow, somewhat excited for a semi-retired oldie.

Sunday dawned, the famous English breakfast was consumed, and I drove to the Science Park to pick up *The Waverley*. The sun shone brightly in an azure blue sky and the paddle steamer looked majestic nestled up against the quay the sun reflecting from her two red white and black funnels and her white topping.

There was a good crowd going on board. I estimated some 450 or so passengers, a mixture of mums dads, children, grandmas and granddads plus steamer buffs like me. We set sail at 10 am and initially a family with two lads sat next to me so we started chatting. They were on holiday and the lads were very excited: dad was too. Mum? Well mum was mum. Ha! I explained my interest and gave them the benefit or otherwise of my vast knowledge of *The Waverley*. Zzzzzzzzz!

I decided to wander around the ship and get a coffee and so said cheerio and hoped we would bump into each other later.

Sunday lunch on *The Waverley* is famous and with either turkey/beef, roast potatoes, new potatoes, Yorkshire pudding and gravy, plus two veg. And all for £8.50. Wow! Who could say no? Imagine my surprise when I sat down to eat and the family I first met on board came over to join me.

We began to chat about where they lived: Southport, which is also where I lived. They told me that they had moved into a lovely house with a large pond in the garden but, as the two boys where very young then, they had filled it in.

'It's strange', they said, 'because many a time we feel like we are being watched. The boys feel people in the side passage and they say they can sometimes hear whispering and a jangling of chains.'

They also claimed on one occasion to have heard a loud splash but the pond was filled in and the next door neighbours, who did have an outside pool, where away on holiday. Anyway, the hard cover had been over the pool.

This was not oppressive but just subtle feelings from time to time. Then, two years ago, it all stopped, the slight atmosphere went, no more feelings of being watched. How odd, I thought.

'You still happy living there?', I asked them.

'Oh yes, always have been. We love the house. Inside it is homely, cosy and a great feeling of togetherness; we've always loved it. It is just the odd feeling when we are outside and usually when sat under the umbrella on a sunny day having a barbeque and a drink or two.'

They asked me where I had lived and I told them. Their mouths opened wide but words failed to come out.

'Are you OK?' I asked.

'Well yes, but we've just realised. It's your house we bought!'

I was dumbfounded.

The reason we moved, I explained, was that my eldest son was diagnosed with a mental illness, schizo-affective disorder with psychotic episodes. He had attempted suicide five or six times and had been sectioned many times. He had spent most of his adult life in and out of hospital, low secure units or day units but had always been placed in flats as we could not cope with him living with us.

He regularly came home for showers and meals and, when he was going downhill, we would take him in and nurse him in conjunction with his team of psychiatrists and CPN (community psychiatric nurse). Often we had to have him sectioned. As parents this used to be heart-breaking as 'the gang' that would arrive consisted of four or five police officers, a psychiatrist, his GP, an approved social worker and usually his CPN too.

What I found uncanny was one occasion that still sticks in our memory. It was a lovely sunny day and we were in the back garden, sipping cool cordials. Sat round the table were my wife, me, my son the approved social worker and my son's psychiatrist. The police had been called and five of them were waiting down the side passage quietly in case anything should take off.

(I must point out that my son was very robust, fit and someone who you would not want to mess with. Hence the five large Bobbies.)

The psychiatrist explained to my son that he was about to be sectioned. My son leapt up like lightning, grabbed the psychiatrist by his tie, pulled him across the grass and threw him into the pond, with a resounding splash.

Meanwhile the constabulary rushed round from the passageway and jumped on my son and handcuffed him. He was then taken off to hospital. Two years ago, following twenty years of drug abuse, smoking sixty plus a day, and alcohol, he passed away with a form of cancer.

They just looked at me in total shock. Both they and I would remember our trip on *The Waverley* for absolutely awesome reasons. I still cannot believe the coincidences. We promised to keep in touch.

- 19 -

A Tandem and a Baby

It is July 1959 and as Bobby Darin, Cliff Richard and The Drifters compete for the airwaves, Harold McMillan is the Conservative Prime Minister, UK postcodes are introduced, Juke Box Jury is first shown on TV, hemlines are just above the knee, a little family story unfolds in the depths of Ilford.

My Mum and Dad were married in October 1957 and had moved in with nice Aunty Rose and Uncle Walter and their house in Mortlake Road, Ilford. Mum and Dad had one room downstairs, one up and a box room off the bedroom all situated at the front of the house.

Aunty Rose and Uncle Walter's daughter, Iris had these rooms before and during the War (WWII) as the previous occupants had been bombed out of their own place in Upton Park (just down the road).

The house had three big bedrooms a box room upstairs, a kitchen downstairs and a small garden. Mum was 26 and Dad was 23 (nearly).

My Dad's brother, Louis, had a tandem bike but once he married, it was left behind and Dad 'acquired' it when he came out of the Navy, (after doing his National Service), and he and Mum were married.

Acquiring things became one of my Dad's life skills. It was always 'freemans' or 'buckshee' this basically meant he didn't pay for it and either found it or rescued it from the roadside or the tip. My first typewriter was one such rescue. It was a Remington manual (yes, I did say, manual) typewriter that someone was getting rid of at the tip. I was 12 at the time and consequently learnt to type. A fridge freezer came my way much later, complete with ice.

It was pretty uncommon in 1959 to own a tandem and although most people had bikes, Mum couldn't ride one. A tandem was another matter, however, and much easier, at least according to my Dad, who managed to persuade her so.

Tandems date back to 1898 and were used in the second Anglo Boer War. The UK Tandem Club was founded in 1971. In order to utilise the correct and appropriate tandem terminology, the rider at the front is termed the Captain, Pilot or Steersman, the rider to the rear is referred to as the Stoker, Navigator or Rear Admiral. Now you know.

Mum and Dad decided to go on holiday on a tandem on the cheap. They found out Mum was pregnant in June and the baby expected in February.

They were interested in the Youth Hostel Association – it provided reasonably priced holiday accommodation as they were saving up to buy their own first house. In the past they'd been to holiday camps but this year they wanted to re-visit Somerset, where Mum had been evacuated to during the War in 1940 and to see the Cheddar Gorge.

Mum could just manage to ride on the back of the tandem. The YHA was one of the cheapest forms of holidaying and the tandem one of the cheapest form of transport – so it was a marriage made in heaven, or Ilford at the very least.

In 1958 Mum and Dad managed a trial run on the tandem. They had 'tandemmed' to Bury St Edmunds for a short holiday to Aunty Pat and Uncle Claude's at Stanton. Mum said it was 'OK'.

One of the rules of the YHA was that you had to arrive either by bicycle, by walking, or by water, but not public transport. Youth Hostelling as a concept began in Germany in 1909 with the ethos, 'get to love your homeland and you'll love it more'. Hitler banned youth hostelling in 1936 – having his own ideas about travelling abroad. It would not be for another twenty years until Great Britain embraced the youth hostelling ideal.

The YHA declared that the country was still coming to terms with the fall-out of war and the austerity imposed along with the horrors. Young people needed a chance to get out and enjoy the countryside.

The tandem had two army haversacks situated either side of the back wheel behind Mum. These haversacks could be locked in the dorm at the Hostel when they were out and about.

They arranged to send a parcel of their clothing to the Hostel in Somerset ahead of their arrival, so they didn't have to carry so much.

Mum and Dad saved up hard to pay for the cost of their meals and stay at the Hostel in advance. These costs came to the princely sum of half a crown. This money they sent on in advance of their stay.

To put some perspective on this arrangement, a shilling was 5 pence in old money (before Decimalisation), now worth 77 pence. Half a crown was 2 shillings and sixpence, or 12½ pence or £1.44 today. Sixpence was worth about 28 pence in our money.

So when you could get breakfast for one shilling and sixpence and an evening meal for half a crown, you know it's good value, the term rip-off Britain was yet to be invented.

Packing for the trip into the haversacks consisted of: sleeping bag liners (two), t-shirts, raincoat, clean socks and pants. That would be about it.

Dad took the map and was in front, you can call him the Captain, etc. Mum brought up the rear, she can be the navigator. The map was not just any old map, this was a Youth Hostel map that detailed all the hostels on.

Mum and Dad began their trek between 9.00 am and 10.00 am from Ilford on the Saturday, five miles from the London Overground at Beacontree Station. This was to be their one holiday of the year and had been much anticipated, researched and planned and planned.

They averaged between 20 and 25 miles per day. Their first journey took them from Ilford to Maidenhead in Berkshire. The Hostel was named Jordans. Dad said the traffic around the North Circular was a difficult negotiation but both he and Mum were so excited, they knew it was a big undertaking and felt just like pioneers!

Thus they arrived at their first stop, tired, worn out and dispirited as they couldn't get a meal as it was the first night of their trip that they hadn't realised was a self-catered one. So both saddle-sore in the very truest sense, Mum set about foraging in the hostel kitchen as there were supplies there. Mum purchased a small array of tins from the hostel shop and from this she fashioned a kind of stew (her words, not mine). The stew had some tin of meat and some beans and was lovingly entitled a one-pot wonder.

As this was 1959 and although they had been married for nearly two years, Youth Hostel regulations being what they were, forbade mixed accommodation. So my Mum and Dad were separated for the night. They kissed on the stairs and Dad went off to the boy's dormitory and Mum to the girls.

In the morning, Mum and Dad met their fellow Hostellers. About 10 people, mainly young, no children (they obviously didn't know about Mum's bun). Youth Hostels didn't accept children staying at the time.

Breakfast was a communal affair, with a bell to awaken you and chores apportioned to guests. These chores would be general household duties, such as floor sweeping, taking the rubbish out and cleaning up of the kitchen.

Youth Hostels are still in existence however, unlike those in 1959, guests can pull up in their cars with their children and rent family accommodation. Did you know the youth tourist market is now worth £15 billion per year?

After breakfast and only once your chores had been completed, was it back on the tandem and onto the road for the next stage. This next stage of the Tour de England was to Hungerford (on the edge of Berkshire).

Once arrived at Hungerford, there was a full evening meal and breakfast but you still had to pay your way (so to speak) and the chore regime continued.

Thus it was from Hungerford the trusty steed took Mum and Dad to Bath. However, halfway along the road, the rain began to fall, the two of them were soaked to the skin in their shorts and plimsolls. They were able to put the tandem in the Guard's van of the train at Marlborough and travel in relative comfort in a typical English summer.

The train took them to Bath where they disembarked and had to locate the Hostel. This hostel was set at the bottom of a large hill nestled into the hill itself with a river and the most stunning of scenery.

When asked what they spoke about during the journeys, Mum and Dad said that conversation was limited, due to the logistics of the tandem set up. It would mostly consist of Dad asking Mum to 'put your arm out for a left turn, pedal faster or shall we stop for a shandy?'

Their abiding memories were those of the soreness of miles and miles of tandemming. To this day Mum hasn't ridden a bike but my Dad rode one to and from work each day for years and still rides his push-bike to the allotment.

One family story I have is that when my Dad was looking for work around 1966 or thereabouts, he got on his bike saying to Mum, I shall be back when I've found a job. He did and he was. My Dad was the inspiration for the Tory cheer 'on yer bike' I'm sure. Two Normans in a pod.

During the Tour de England, Mum and Dad were overtaken mainly by buses and the occasional lorries. Our road system wasn't nearly as clogged as it is today with the M6 car park as it's affectionately known. In 1959 there were way fewer private cars and Mum and Dad had the quiet country lanes mostly to themselves.

As a consequence of their forced evening separations, Mum would get into conversation with the other girls staying at the Hostel. Actually, this is a true talent of my Mum. She has the ability to engage almost everyone, even teenagers, in conversation. I wouldn't say anything that mentioned donkeys or hind legs at all!

On one such occasion, Mum got talking with a group of girls who had just arrived whilst they were putting their pyjamas under the pillows. The girls Mum spoke with didn't arrive by bike, they'd hitchhike their way between Hostels, some of them coming from Scotland.

They would wait in a café for the lorry drivers to leave and, after ascertaining the driver's destinations and willingness to take passengers, they'd travel in the cab with the driver. Once they'd got to where they were going, the lorry driver often stood the girls a meal, lunch, etc.

The girls told my Mum that they didn't want to give away anything more than mealtime companionship and would escape out of the toilet windows and look for their next lift. To my Mum, who was older than these girls, (her being a married pregnant lady of 26 and they being in their late teens) these tales were horror stories and she said to them, 'But that's so dangerous, anything could happen!' To which they strenuously denied that it would and all would be OK.

Sadly this wasn't always true. A girl had been murdered in Scotland that same year and only recently it being all over the news. It would seem that nothing changes, does it?

Whilst Mum and Dad were in Bath, they caught a bus to Weston-super-Mare then onto Wookey Hole.

They stayed in Bath for a few days, the Hostel being located in the centre of Bath and they enjoyed the opportunity to walk (not ride!) get the bus to Bath and soak up the sights, the Crescent, the Pump Room and a look at the baths. They walked along the beach at Weston-super-Mare, had lunch and ice-cream (probably two, knowing my Mum!) then back to the Hostel for their communal evening meal and chores.

In the evenings they'd sit in the lounge, talking and drinking coffee until lights out at 9.30 pm – such hedonism! It was always an early start in the morning. You could elect for either evening or morning chores, but not no chores. Guests (although that seems an elaborate term for cheapish labour) would also be expected to help prepare the meals.

From Bath it was thence to Cheddar Gorge. Earlier in year, Cheddar Gorge had been closed due to flooding but Mum and Dad became the first people to ride through the Gorge on their bike after it opened again.

Mum and Dad fondly recall whizzing down from the top of the gorge (no cars were allowed at that time due to the flooding) right through to the bottom to the village. Cheddar Gorge at its height is about 449 feet! Dad remembers wondering, and hoping, that the brakes were going to hold rather than sending them careening over the edge. They both loved the feeling of thrill and exhilaration of feeling like the only two people alive, free-wheeling down along with no traffic nor people at all.

They stayed in Cheddar for about 2 days, time enough time to visit the place where Mum had been evacuated in that war-torn time 19 years before – Wookey Hole. They talked with Mrs Rose who first took Mum in.

Mrs Rose didn't recognise Mum at first until she said, 'You probably don't remember me, but I'm your little evacuee'. They then had a tour down Mum's memory-lane of the village Post Office and pub and the school.

My parents try to go back each year to pay their respects in a way to those families who took in the children of London all those years ago. Mum remarked that throughout the trip she was mercifully free of morning sickness.

They remember peddling as being hot, thirsty and tiring work. They'd often look for a stream to paddle their weary feet in or wait outside pubs until they opened to get their shandies.

They both agreed it was so much faster than walking and with the added bonus of pulling the tandem to one side of the road to rest, soak up the scenery, paddle their feet and enjoy the sights such as the white horse by Salisbury Plain, Stonehenge and Glastonbury.

Then it was on the A30 back into London and towards home only to bump into their future brother-in-law. 'Funny,' they said, 'you go all that way and back again and who do you bump into, but family!' It took 6 days to get there with 3 days in Cheddar itself and 6 days to get back.

From the family photo album, here's my Mum and Dad and here's the famous tandem, it would seem that yes, 'they can ride tandem'.

When asked how much they had enjoyed that holiday, they said that 50 years of time passing couldn't hope to erase the fond memories! Then, on the 13th February 1960, a bouncing baby boy 'pedalled' his way into this world.

- 20 -

Away from Home

Having not had the opportunity to travel much while growing up, I was delighted when my eldest child came home from school one day and informed me that he had been one of the pupils in his school chosen to go on a trip to Spain.

It was quite an expensive trip but he is a good boy who works hard at school and I would not deprive him of this experience. Also, the main thing was I didn't want him to miss out on anything, as I had. As you can imagine, he was over the moon when I told him he could go. (His younger brother was not so impressed but he would soon have the same opportunity.)

Weeks of planning and over-excitement passed. My son was extremely ecstatic, as the school had informed them that day that they had managed to secure a visit to Camp Nou, the home football stadium to FC Barcelona. To a young lad of fifteen, this was a dream come true.

His excitement was overwhelming, much to the annoyance of his three younger siblings. The days could not pass enough for my boy.

Finally, after almost getting no sleep all night, the morning came where myself and my wife were to take him to school to begin his journey to his 'once in a lifetime opportunity' as he called it.

We were told to arrive at school for 11.00 am, as the coaches were due to leave at midday. Typical of my son, and despite weeks of nagging from his mother, he decided that the best time to pack for a week away in another country would be 9.00 am the very same morning!

As I say, his mother and even I had tried to urge him to pre-pack, but I guess at that age, packing is not a priority. My wife and I were a little annoyed with his laid back, disorganised attitude, but we refrained from saying anything as we didn't want to burst his bubble.

At 10.25 am he was finally ready. After a quick bye to his two younger brothers and his younger sister, he scurried out of the front door telling his mother and me that it would be our fault if he were to miss the 11.00 am deadline. The need to slowly count to ten was occurring.

We arrived at the school gates on time. Two huge coaches were parked, surrounded by a sea of Year 10 and Year 11 students, all accompanied by their parents, who, I must add, looked how I felt – nervous, anxious, happy and very stressed.

After numerous head counts by the teachers, it was time for my son to take his seat on his designated coach. This would be his first trip away from home. I tried to remain calm and macho, even though deep down inside I was feeling very emotional and somewhat scared. To my right, it was a different story, my wife could not hide her emotions and was in floods of tears, much to the embarrassment of my son! Mothers and sons, eh!

He shook my hand, whilst his mother opted to kiss him on the forehead (something he tried greatly to avoid) and off he went. I watched my not so little boy excitedly join his friends, laughing and joking. Off they set for an agonising 26 hour coach trip from wet Solihull to sunny Barcelona.

The journey consisted of a drive to the Port of Dover, where they would board a ferry to arrive at France and then continue from France all the way to Spain and eventually Barcelona. I was intrigued as to how he would pass the time, but he had taken various entertainment items/consoles/gadgets with him and I was pretty certain that whilst with his friends the time would fly by.

A week passed and much to the relief of my wife and I he had returned home safe and sound. He was still buzzing with excitement and was eager to tell me what he had been up to…

'Dad, Dad! It was THE best time of my life! Thank you so much for letting me go. The journey was sooooo long, on the way there so I played Street Fighter on my phone but the battery died, so then I watched some DVDs, then me and the boys played some games, and then we slept. I was sharing a room with Jake and Karl and we had so much fun!

'The first day wasn't that good as we stayed in the hotel unpacking and just getting settled. But Dad the second day was the best ever. We went to Camp Nou, Barcelona's football stadium. I saw the dressing rooms of the team, particularly Messi, Xavi and Iniesta! Dad it was the most surreal moment of my life so far and to know that I was standing in the same spot as those footballers was just unbelievable!

'Then we went to some historic museums, wine gardens and theme parks. That was good fun! They were all great experiences. Then we went to Las Ramblas, on the last day. This was like a large pavement in the middle of the street, not at the side but in the middle and the roads and shops were either side. I saw all sorts of things here Dad, there was one man impersonating Ronaldinho walking backwards up a ladder all whilst performing kick ups! It was quite wacky! Dad it was crazy and me Jake and Karl did almost think it really was Ronaldinho! Then there was this man and woman who were pretending to be statues and scaring passers-by. They didn't fool me and my mates though, we were too clever for them! We spent about four hours at Las Ramblas as it was just so interesting to see all the different things that were going on. It was just unbelievable. We went to the shops there too. There were lots of shops selling imitation football gear but I didn't buy anything as I knew that you and mom wouldn't want me wasting money on overpriced fake items! Jake did though, he said he didn't care if his Dad would shout...'

After all his excitement, he finally came up for air and realised he was exhausted and needed to shower and get a good night's sleep in the comfort of his own home. It was so endearing to listen to his stories and I was certain that there were many more to tell, he just didn't have the energy at that time. He had experienced Spanish culture, visited some famous land marks and stood in the same spot as his beloved football team. In his words 'this was the greatest experience of his life'.

- 21 -

Echoes from the Past

'Do you believe in ghosts?'

It was an odd question to have been fired at me by an ageing and ailing theologian during my Oxford entrance interview.

Quite what it had to do with the law degree I hoped to undertake was less than apparent although I suspected, due to his grey complexion, sunken eyes and persistent hacking cough, that my interrogator was perhaps seeking some reassurance of a continued existence after death.

No doubt the question was designed to see how well I handled something unexpected, something that no interview technique handbook was able to prepare you for. I presume that the reaction the five esteemed academics seated in front of me anticipated was a confusion of 'umm' and 'err' and then a stumbling analysis of how the absence of sound evidence would preclude the 'beyond a reasonable doubt' verdict as to their existence.

So they struggled to prevent a perfectly synchronised raising of five sets of eyebrows when I immediately and very certainly answered, 'Yes, of course.'

'Oh, really? Please explain why,' came the eventual reply. And so my story began.

I had the privilege to grow up in a large country house, set in the Cheshire countryside with a quaint village at the end of the drive. The hub of village life was, of course, the village pub; picture postcard perfect, with a black and white timbered frame and thatched roof. It had stood its ground since the mid-seventeenth century, the groves in the red sandstone stone step and the nailed oak door worn smooth by countless hands; both testaments to its longevity.

Not that I was a frequent attendee of the pub. I was six. My knowledge of it was based firmly on what I could see from the car when we emerged from between the tall brick pillars and heavy gates which guarded the entrance to the drive. As I swept past on the way to school or shopping I would occasional catch a glimpse of a dark and mysterious interior, often thick with smoke from either the patrons or the coal fire that constantly belched dark grey clouds from the crooked brick chimney.

The house I lived in was supposedly haunted. My father had told me that a previous inhabitant was reported to walk the upper corridors at night, dragging chains behind him and moaning – the stuff of pantomime or Scooby Doo. I'd never heard or seen him. I'd also been told of the disembodied voice of a maid who was supposed to cry out 'I was pushed!' when you visited the top landing on the main staircase. She had apparently met her demise at the bottom of the stairs, a fall of a considerable distance. Again, no such auditory allegations had ever troubled me.

Being the youngest of three brothers, I'd had all the usual childhood myths like Santa Claus and the Tooth Fairy shattered from an early age. So I was, in a six-year-old way, sceptical.

On 9th November, a crisp almost winter night, as I approached my seventh birthday, I was getting ready for bed. The bedtime routine was not one to linger over in the winter. A combination of the 1970s energy crisis, a central heating system that deserved its own Preservation Order as a piece of industrial heritage and ceiling so high that the step ladders to hang the curtains had to be specially made meant that it was bitingly cold. Often I woke to find that the moisture from my breath had condensed onto the bedding overnight and then frozen stiff.

As I washed my hands and face the light in the bathroom suddenly went out. That was nothing unusual; the wiring was even older than the heating. What struck me was that the room was not plunged into darkness but remained brightly lit. The curtains were open and a full moon shone outside but I had to crane my neck from the east facing window to see it fully.

I decided to look at it from the window in the adjoining room, which was on the north facing wall of a tower that overlooked the cobbled courtyard. As the sash slid upwards I was greeted with a fantastic view of a moon that appeared far too big for the sky; it hung just over the roof of the stable block. I felt I could pick out features on the moon's surface as if I had a telescope. The night was so bright I could see all the yard and buildings below me in perfect detail.

As I glanced down I saw a man and a dog enter the courtyard from the left, through the gates that had never been closed to my knowledge. He was oddly dressed with heavy boots, long socks trousers that stopped just below his knees, a leather waistcoat with a pale rough shirt underneath and a three-pointed hat (or a 'tricorne' as I later came to know). I couldn't make out his face as it was in the shadow of the hat brim but he seemed to be looking down and talking to the dog.

The dog itself was a small lively animal of indeterminate breed. Although it was running around the man's feet, and I could see its muzzle opening and closing as if barking, I heard nothing from the man or dog.

As the pair of them reached the last stable door of the main block they simply vanished. There was no cloud over the moon, no sudden gust of wind to cause me to blink, they just disappeared. I watched the courtyard for a few more minutes to see if they were in a shadow somewhere but nothing stirred.

My concern was that someone was in the courtyard and might be trying to break in so I hurried downstairs to tell my father. Being a man who came to fatherhood somewhat late in life he was not exactly energetic, especially after dinner and a glass of port. So I was not surprised when he didn't jump to his feet, grab a shotgun from the gun room and rush out to investigate. Instead he listened carefully to my description of what I'd seen and then smiled curiously.

'Follow me,' he said and led me to the library. Reaching up to what seemed like an impossibly high shelf (I was only six remember) he pulled down a large, brown, leather bound book which I had never seen before. In a clichéd flourish he blew dust from the top edge. The book was a history of the village and had been written by the local vicar in the late 1800s.

He studied the inner pages for a few moments before thumbing through to the middle portion and, after a few minutes of reading and page turning, he handed me the book and placed a finger on the start of a paragraph.

'Read that,' was all he said.

What I read (admittedly with my father's assistance on some of the longer and more arcane words) was an account of a groom at the house who, on returning from the pub late one night with his dog, was trampled to death by a horse that hadn't been tethered properly in its stable. The belief was that the horse had bolted after becoming frightened by the barking of the groom's dog. He had died, along with his dog who suffered the same fate, on November 9th 1775.

As I finished my tale and looked around the interviewing panel I had a sudden horrifying realisation that my account, and lack of logical reasoning or analysis as to what I saw, had not impressed them. Despite my best efforts to dig myself out of the hole I was in, you will not be surprised to hear that I failed the interview. And, despite returning to the same window at the same time on the same day for several years afterwards, I never did see the ghost again.

- 22 -

The Mystery Room

It was a family gathering for the christening of my wife's niece approximately e years ago. My wife's sister, Julia, thought that her cottage was too small to accommodate everyone for the day, so her mother-in-law agreed to use her house. It is a large farmhouse which apparently dates back to the thirteenth century.

On arrival, and after the christening, my wife and I and our eight-month-old daughter joined the other guests in the kitchen at the farmhouse. After a short while Emma recalls a small announcement that we should use the family bathroom at the front of the house 'when the need arises'.

When the need did arise, Emma went to use the family bathroom which was unusually large and the floor sloped in line with the age of the house. There was a door in the bathroom that was slightly ajar and, being nosey, she looked inside. She saw that it was an on-suite bedroom with a wrought iron bed and a bedside cabinet. The bed was neatly made and the room was furnished in an orderly fashion, in keeping with the age and style of the house.

She went downstairs and told her middle sister, Lisa, what she had found, thinking that it would have been of interest to her husband, who was a builder and enjoyed renovating houses. They agreed that next time one of them needed the bathroom they would go together and take another look.

A short while later, our baby daughter's nappy needed changing, so Emma decided to take her sister with her to change the baby. Lisa liked the sloping bathroom and thought it was very unique and noticed that the door to the 'other room' had been closed. Emma presumed that Julia's mother-in-law had been in the room and closed the door for privacy.

They both decided to open the door and look inside because Lisa was intrigued as to its contents. When they opened the door it was no more than an airing cupboard. Emma was totally shocked, but Lisa said that she did believe what Emma had seen.

When they went downstairs and told people of their encounter, Emma was told that she must have been mistaken and that she had probably had too much wine. She recalled that she hadn't 'touched a drop' because she was responsible for our young daughter at the time and would never 'drink on duty'.

The experience played on Emma's mind for some time. On visiting Julia a few weeks later, she told her the story. Julia laughed at first and then suddenly recalled a memory that struck a chord. She took Emma to the old cider-mill on the farm (where the house stands) which had since been used for storage and she asked Emma if she recognised anything. Leaning against the wall, was the head and foot of the wrought iron bed that Emma had seen in the bedroom. Julia told her that those items had been stored in the cider-mill for years and hadn't been touched for as long as she could remember.

On regaling the story to Julia's mother-in-law, who had lived in the house all of her life, she was told that there used to be a room in the house with that bed in, where the vet would stay, many years ago, when he attended to sheep and cattle at night in bad weather. She also told Emma that some time afterwards, the room was had been converted into smaller rooms, leaving the door in the bathroom to simply open into an airing cupboard. There was, apparently, no way that anyone alive today could have known about the room. Needless to say, Emma hasn't been back since.

- 23 -

Leave Us Alone!

This is a real life experience which I assure you is not a made-up story. Many year ago if someone had told me that I would have witnessed something so unreal, I would have said: 'Are you kidding me? Where is the camera?' But now, even though people might lie, I would believe them.

The strangest experience of my life happened 20 years ago (give or take) when I was at university, sharing a flat with my brother. It was our first year and the flat we have moved in was a new one.

At the beginning it was a peaceful place and the location of the flat was very sought after, so we felt very lucky to be able get it. Most of our neighbours were university lecturers.

After a normal month, things started changing inside the house, gradually. First, both of us started seeing a black shadow passing very fast across the entrance hall in such a way that 'It' (whatever 'It' was) did not seem to mind our existence. Of course, it was only after a while that we confessed to each other what we had seen.

Then lights started to turn on and off infrequently; the TV and the CD player would turn on or off also and the CD inside the player would change to Pink Floyd each time when we left the house. Most importantly, things have started going missing. At first, most of these events we were putting as mishap or simply coincidence.

One night just after we drifted off to sleep, I felt cold and woke up. My brother was still asleep at the next room. Two or three minutes later I started hearing a guitar sound coming from our lounge. My brother must have woken up. He started calling my name out. I shouted back to him saying that 'I can hear it too'.

Slowly we both got out of the bed and walked to the living room. We were so frightened we could not talk. My knees were all wobbly. However, I knew we had to go there and face the reality, no matter what the outcome.

We arrived at the doorway: the sound was definitely coming from our living room. I reached out to the light switch and turned it on. Immediately, the music stopped but we could see that the guitar strings were still vibrating and that the guitar was on the sofa, not at its usual place in the corner of the room leaning on the wall.

That was it. From that point forward we knew we were not alone. Someone or something was also living with us but we were not sure if 'It' was friendly or evil. Not long afterwards the house's atmosphere turned angry.

I should add here that it came to a point where we were not the only two people experiencing all these things. 'It' was not hesitating to reveal itself to others. All our friends who visited us would see or hear something odd.

Once the freakiest things happened in front of three of our friends, all of whom already knew about the ghost. While I and one of friend were cooking in the kitchen, the other people, including my brother, were sitting and waiting for dinner. After chopping some tomatoes I left the knife on my right side at the work top. Then the knife started spinning. We were all shocked, frozen and, frankly, freaked out.

After almost half a minute, the knife stopped but then before we could turn in to our normal states one of the girls got up and started singing and dancing. Clearly she was possessed by the ghost.

Once she stopped, she opened her mouth wide, facing towards the ceiling and let the ghost to leave her body. Then she started crying and shivering. She was saying 'I am very cold and I do not know the reason'.

After that last event we decided to find a medium and get rid of the ghost. None of us was sure whether 'It' was a good natured ghost or a mean one.

After a couple of days of asking everyone, we found a boy, who was only seventeen, who could see things and talk to them. We called him and booked a session.

The boy's house was in a village and even to get there was eventful. The drive was two hours long but we reached there after five hours of a long hassled drive. First the day was all shiny and bright but as soon as we entered the woodland which was leading to his house, the thunder and lightning started.

There was a terrible rain blocking our vision for driving so we had to stop for about an hour. Then Koral, who was driving the car, ran over a fox. That is was not the last thing.

Ten minutes later we had a flat tyre. When we arrived the boy knew all of this and said to us, 'I know it was difficult to come here but I am glad you did'. He also added, 'I assure you all will be better soon.' And it was.

During our session we found out that our building was on top of an old graveyard. The ghost in our flat was a young and playful girl. She was not harmful or dangerous in any way at all. She was only enjoying watching our scared faces.

When we went back to our house we were all calmer. We slept well that night without any disturbance from the ghost. We were told if she did something scary we should tell her to stop, which we all did. Gradually the house was all quiet and peaceful again except the parties we had after the exams.

There was one last incident which seemed to stop all the weirdness. I was getting ready to go to class. All the others were waiting at the door and telling me to speed up.

I looked at the mirror one last time to check myself and then I saw her. She was stood right behind me and looking at me through the mirror. I must admit she was the prettiest thing I had ever seen. She had a naughty smile on her face and so I smiled back. I turned to see her but she was not there. Since then neither I, nor any other person in the same flat, has never seen her or witnessed anything scary. That was it. It was her way of saying goodbye. She was gone. Although I now know the truth about her, I don't think I will ever miss her...

- 24 -

The Story of Betty Thornton

Betty Thornton was born in an upstairs bedroom of a terrace house in the Hyde Park area of Leeds, and went on to Art College in Bradford. However, she ended up befriending the President of Botswana and then going on to get to know one of the twentieth century's greatest icons – Princess Diana – and looked after her and Prince Charles on the first few days after their wedding. This is her story.

February 1926 saw Betty come in to the world in the house of George and Dorothy Foster, in Hyde Park, near the centre of Leeds. Her father was a buyer for the wool industry in Bradford, and her mother built a family home which was to influence Betty throughout her life, especially the early fascination she developed with cooking good traditional food as the centre piece to meals where conversation was king.

Her real skills were in art and, after schooling in Pudsey, she went on to Bradford College of Art and Textile Design. Here she met her future husband, John Thornton who went on to be a respected classical sculptor.

Marriage changed the whole direction of Betty's life. After college in Bradford, John got a prestigious place at Chelsea Art College and this meant the big move down to London. Following the war accommodation in London was very difficult to get but they managed to get a small flat on Adolphus Road.

It so happened that in the neighbouring flat was Seretse Khama and his wife Ruth Williams. At the time their love affair was the biggest news story there was, as he was the chief of the Bamangwato Tribe in Bechuanaland (present day Botswana), and he had met a white girl. This was a time when mixed marriages were generally frowned upon, let alone for a future African King.

When they got married there was horror in many parts of the world, especially neighbouring South Africa, which had Apartheid. Khama's own tribe, led by his Uncle Tshkedi, tried to stop the marriage. Even the British Government became heavily involved through the Commonwealth.

Outside the flat the press were camped, waiting for a view of the couple. Betty used to regularly dress up as Ruth to act as a decoy for the press so she and Seretse could get out of the flat and spend some time together.

Ruth and Betty became lifelong friends, even after they moved back to Botswana. Seretse had to give up his inherited right to be King but his people voted him to be their first President.

With her husband John pursuing a career as an artist and sculptor, it fell to Betty to become the bread winner. She fell back on her love of cooking and made a career that was to place her in to the company of film stars and royalty.

After humble beginnings, her work moved up to a whole new level when, in 1979, she was taken on by the family of Lord Mountbatten of Burma, shortly after he had been murdered by the IRA. This was at a house called Broadlands and her new employer was into film. This meant the house was continually full of famous film stars such as Peter Ustinov, David Niven, James Mason as well as many famous jazz musicians.

Other famous guests were, of course, the Royal Family, and especially Prince Charles who had been very close to his Uncle, Lord Mountbatten. It was during this time that Prince Charles had met Lady Diana Spencer and the couple did much of their courting in the secure grounds at Broadlands.

The Royal Family are very easy going when on their own and Lady Diana would often sit around the kitchen table and talk to Betty. Through this connection Betty would be invited to Buckingham Palace. Betty still has her food itineraries from the shooting seasons in 1980 and 1981, when the guests were The Queen and Prince Philip, Countess Mountbatten of Burma, The King and Queen of Greece, Clive Aston, Mr and Mrs Evelyn de Rothschild, and more.

The 29th July 1981, however was to become the most important day in Betty's working life. A few months before it had been decided that Prince Charles and Lady Diana Spencer would spend the first few days of their honeymoon at Broadlands and Betty, the butler, footmen and housekeeper, would be the only people there to look after them.

Betty was sworn to secrecy for the months beforehand and she spent her time planning what was to be eaten and when during this stay. Of course, she was familiar with the personal likes of the royal couple and accordingly planned everything in advance.

On the day that 900 million viewers around the world were watching the fairytale wedding, Betty was also watching it on the television but in the kitchen at Broadlands, knowing that in no time at all she would have the greatest honour of her life.

Everything was ready for the first meal which had been set up on paved veranda at the back of the house overlooking the River Test.

On the television the world watched the cars carrying the royal couple drive through the gates at Broadlands and then close shut. Betty made her way to the front door and, as the cars pulled up, opened the door and had the honour of welcoming the newly married couple to Broadlands for their honeymoon.

She curtseyed and said, 'Welcome your Royal Highnesses.' And Charles replied, 'Isn't Diana beautiful? I am the luckiest man. How did it all look? Has Vic (the butler) got it on video?'

Of the many memories she has of that day, she remembers Charles and Diana walking arm-in-arm down by the river and, on the veranda, Charles serenading Diana with a song.

After Broadlands, Betty went on to work for a family outside Uttoxeter, and then at Daylesford in Gloucestershire. Betty worked until retiring and is now back in her beloved Bradford, where she had lived as a child, then studied and met her beloved John.

- 25 -

The Flying Squad?

Sitting in the garden in the garden on one of the last of summer's balmy days, sipping a kir and gently putting the world to rights with an old friend. The dog's trying to get at the rabbits in the field beyond, or jump on an emergent mole, and all was as peaceful as it could be in this sleepy part of Norfolk.

Suddenly, mass barking erupted and the five bar gate creaked. We were enjoying the peace and quiet, and wickedly hoped that the intruder would go away and not spot us; but then the crunching of footsteps on gravel made us realize that an interruption was going to take place. Dressed in gardening shorts, a T-shirt and flip flops I ambled up to greet the uninvited guest.

A middle aged lady appeared.

'Hallo!' She said. 'My cousin has just died in the States and although we were not very close, his elderly father has given me a task. After the War my cousin flew a plane in Norfolk and he then hid it in a barn in the area around his local watering hole, which is down the road. Do you own the farm? Which are your barns? Is there a plane around here without a propeller – or maybe you have a spare propeller in your barn?' She then drew breath. I was speechless and wished that she had been too.

She did not budge and was revelling in a story about her having been a police officer between 1976 and 1984. Furthermore, she was good detective! I could only stand and marvel at her modesty. Gradually I learned that her husband, more recently retired from the police force, was having nothing to do with 'her enquiries'. Again, lost for words, I could only smile and nod.

The three labradors bounded onto the scene and were soon making friends in their boisterous manner.

My heart was in my mouth thinking she'd have me under the Dangerous Dogs Act – even though I knew full well she was only in danger of being licked to death. By this time she was on a level with my garage - an old barn with a leaky roof – and to my absolute amazement she started inspecting it presumably in the hope of finding an aeroplane or at least a propeller. No such luck.

I began to think I was not going to get rid of this woman and there was the serious business of a kir warming up in the sun, so I propelled her back to the gate but she wouldn't turn around and a sort of ballroom dance ensued. When I took a step forward, she had to take a step backwards and so we tangoed the thirty yards in some five minutes, back to the gate.

How to get rid of her?

There is nothing like telling a good lie, and modesty forbids me telling you just how good I am. I could have claimed insanity, but far better to tell her I was a stranger to the area and had only just moved in.

Shamelessly, I headed her in the direction of my farmer neighbour, telling her he was one of the old boys of the area although I knew him to be a miserable cuss. After a hearty swig of my kir, it amused me to hear her bombarding him with the same tirade of questions. But her visit had a positive side to it; Mr Brown, the farmer concerned, passes up and down past my gate but I never even get a wave from him.

- 26 -

Lazy Sunday Afternoon

Typical quiet Sunday afternoon 'on call' for emergencies. I had been in the hospital all morning and all the loose ends had been tied up, everyone was stable and I was looking forward to a good Sunday lunch, when my emergency trauma bleep shattered the peace.

I called the resus room in the hospital and an anxious sounding nurse answered the phone, and said that they were expecting a 'young female stabbing victim who was being resuscitated at the scene; and she's pregnant'.

It was about a ten minute drive in during which time I had the chance to collect my thoughts and run over procedures in my mind. This sort of thing wasn't that common (thankfully) but the pregnancy held an extra dimension of worry. I had taken the precaution of phoning operating theatres and asking them to meet me in Casualty with an abdominal set, a chest set and vascular instruments, covering all eventualities, or so I thought.

I pushed through the doors of resus to be greeted by the site of a full team carrying out cardiac massage, establishing intravenous lines and generally rushing around organising necessities. It became apparent that the girl in question, who was aged about 21, had been stabbed in the back once with a long thin knife to the medial side of the shoulder blade, and that she was at least 24 weeks pregnant by the size of the bump.

It was also apparent that efforts at resuscitation externally was getting nowhere and the likelihood was that she was still bleeding heavily into the chest cavity. I quickly washed up and gloved without time for transfer to theatre, and cut into the chest from the stab wound forward in the space between the fifth and sixth ribs, releasing a huge volume of liquid and clotted blood.

There was a one inch laceration in the root of the left lung which had by chance divided the main vein and artery to the lung, and these bled profusely with each chest compression. Luckily I had ordered the chest set so could hold the ribs open with a rib retractor whilst I cross clamped the root of the lung with a large vascular clamp, hoping to contain the blood loss and re-establish cardiac activity.

In order to do this I commenced internal compressions of the heart, squeezing it as hard as I could, and regularly enough to circulate the blood efficiently. There are historical accounts of babies being delivered from dead mothers by Caesarean section (supposedly Julius Caesar was born in this fashion) and therefore I asked the gynaecology registrar to deliver the baby. She was initially reluctant but eventually agreed that at least we may have a chance of saving one life. Within 5-7 minutes the baby was out in the open, the paediatric registrar had commenced resuscitation.

We continued internal massage for a further twenty minutes but by general agreement all attempts at resus were stopped and the poor girl was declared dead shortly after, as no signs of life could be established since she had been stabbed. The chances of a single stab wound in the back by an amateur hitting such a vital area are astronomic, but in this instance it was very much a case of wrong place wrong time.

The victim was not supposed to be working that day, but had taken a friends shift at a shop as a favour. The perpetrator had already informed his psychiatric surveillance team that he needed to be stopped as he was intending to stab a woman, a plea that was felt to be a cry for attention as there was no history of violence in his long background of mental illness. It seems it was a single motiveless and pointless attack on a complete stranger which ended in tragedy.

As to the wisdom of persevering with resuscitation on the foetus who had undergone a prolonged period of oxygen starvation, she battled through for the next 10-12 weeks but eventually made it, and was discharged to the care of the grandparents who have at least a small part of their daughter to console them. How she manages in the long term and whether there is any lasting deficit we will not know for a long time but she has a chance and that is more than we could have hoped for.

.

- 27 -

The Desert of Finance

Like all major 'happenings' I can remember the start of it very clearly.

We had just returned to work in January 2007 full of hope and anticipation of a prosperous new year.

In the final run-up to Christmas we had left the workplace in good spirits and an order book that would potentially take us well into the first quarter of that impending new year.

But on the morning of our return that upbeat mood was to change very rapidly as various members of our sales team began to access their e-mails. The number of requests that we had received to put on hold scheduled programmes of production was, to put it mildly, frightening.

Of course at that stage we had no idea as to what was actually behind the unusually high numbers requesting a freeze on production but we were soon to find out!

Further investigation revealed that a number of clients were having their finance restricted or even pulled at the last minute, and with very little warning, by their banks.

This came as a very big shock but it was only the start of things.

By the Spring of 2007 a lot of the big name banks had started a cancellation process that was to reach epidemic proportions – pulling away from commitments that had already been made to businesses up and down the country, giving little or no notice and, of course, no further assistance.

Not only did this leave a lot of our clients in very vulnerable positions but there was an obvious knock-on effect which was starting to impact adversely on our business.

Very quickly we had to rethink our business model. As a company specialising in the manufacture and supply of component parts used by the construction industry, we were operating across Ireland and main UK markets.

The big plc companies were the first to reduce their throughput, and very promptly, but soon others were to follow. Business was drying up and drying up extremely quickly.

We managed to struggle through 2007 maintaining a small output through the local Northern Irish market but we had to radically rethink our strategies, and more importantly, our costings, and that was the beginning of the review to our working week.

In 27 years of doing business, certainly we had encountered challenging market conditions but never before on this scale. And never before had we to consider a reduction to our working week.

It was as if someone had hit a switch!

Within a matter of months we went from being a company that was capable of turning over £10 million annually to a business that was severely struggling and unlikely to achieve even 20% of that figure!

As a business we were finding it difficult to cover our costs. Support was needed like it had never been needed before, but sadly, it wasn't forthcoming. We, like many others, found ourselves in a 'Desert of Finance'.

There was sympathy, but no terms, no oasis and not even the luxury of a mirage! Given the circumstances, I was doing everything I thought I could because, as anyone who has run their own business and who is passionate about it, like I am, will know, you live it 24/7.

With order books decimated, gone were all the basic principles of good business practice you were simply living from day-to-day and with the fear of the unknown.

How long was this all going to last? One year, two years? Did anyone at this stage consider that it might be six years and counting!

Many business owners were facing a dilemma. Bills still had to be paid as had wages and a lot of companies, ourselves included, were finding themselves in a very precarious situation. They wanted to be honest, as we did. That's what our business has been built on – honesty, integrity and accountability.

But here's the crux - by being honest they were incriminating themselves as to their vulnerability and therefore putting themselves at risk. This caused anxiety amongst suppliers and a lot of decent people were left with no alternative but to close shop and suffer the consequences.

Whenever you consider it, this recession, as we all know, has been on a global scale. There are very few people that have not been touched by it as negative equity manifests itself in many different ways.

Advice from the bank was that we needed money and that this should be extracted from our debtors. If only it had been as simple and straightforward as that!

These debtors were either slow to pay or couldn't pay and we had to introduce money into the business by way of loans from family members just to survive. Of course we were fortunate, some might say, to have been in a position to have been able to do that.

But here's the reality. Through no fault of our own we had to reinvest in our own company pouring in hard-earned profits that had been built up over almost three decades of endeavour.

Everyone in business was being asked to look at the value of their assets and to make sure that they were on the right side of their loan to values otherwise the banks would resolve the matter either with you or for you.

To say that I have been scarred by the whole experience is an understatement. So who was to blame for it all?

That's an easy one: the greedy bankers and investment institutions that overstepped the mark. However, governments around the world also had a role to play in all of this.

Banks were lending out money in all kinds of portfolios that were over-stretched and were never going to be paid back. A black hole was created and both individuals and businesses were sucked into it.

Closer to home (and within the UK) the Government practically closed down the construction industry and that impacted greatly, not only on us, but the whole economy.

On numerous occasions Sir Mervyn King called on government to support the sector and ignite the industry, a major contributor to the Treasury. It didn't happen.

But then the Government, like so many others, had run out of money. There was no funding available; austerity had kicked-in and new approaches such as quantitative easing was being looked at as a means of revitalising the economy. Did it work?

The jury is still out on that one but unprecedented times required unprecedented actions. Have I learned any lessons from it all? I most certainly have.

Has the banking fraternity learned any lessons?

I can only say that I hope they have and I can only hope that governments both in the UK and Ireland have learned valuable lessons from all of this. And not only in the UK and Ireland, but globally.

The sad thing is it is people like me who are sharing these experiences and frustrations who will never be in a position to affect change because I for one have no interest in entering the political arena.

However, one thing I am very clear about. We are not in a driving economy, we are in a facilitating economy and we have now all got this bubble resistance that we are mindful of – five years good trading followed by a burst situation.

I can only say from a personal point of view that we have now built in mechanisms to alarm ourselves because we cannot rely on government and we cannot rely on those that we should have been able to rely upon to provide us with the indicators that could have avoided all of this or at least minimised its impact.

In my opinion, direction from government, direction from lending institutions, and from morality institutions didn't exist.

This leads me to accountability. In terms of going forward there has to be some form of accountability.

This whole crisis has most certainly not been without its victims and it causalities but in terms of justice I don't believe there has been any.

With bail outs and pay outs running into millions upon millions of pounds of taxpayers' money is the banking sector worthy of this massive reward for failure?

Sadly, I don't believe the protagonists in all of this will ever be held accountable.

Responsibility is something that you assume, accountability transcends from being a responsible individual and if you are responsible and accountable you are most definitely going to be transparent.

And transparency is something that is very much called for if we are to draw a line in the sand with regards to all of this!

On the positive side of things our business is most definitely on the turn. We can see light at the end of the tunnel. We are back to full working weeks and the order books are at a level that is more than comfortable.

But in terms of a journey it has been a most harrowing one, and one which we most certainly would not like to repeat, which is why it is important that lessons are both learned and applied!